Six of the Best

by
Catharina Elizabeth Roux

Grosvenor House
Publishing Limited

This book is published by
Grosvenor House Publishing Ltd
Link House
140 The Broadway, Tolworth, Surrey, KT6 7HT.
www.grosvenorhousepublishing.co.uk

This book is a work of fiction. Any resemblance to
people or events, past or present, is purely coincidental.

A CIP record for this book
is available from the British Library

ISBN 978-1-83615-249-1

This book is dedicated to my beloved wife and our two incredible sons.

To my wife, your love and support are the foundation of everything I do. To my two boys, you bring light and joy into my life every day. You are my three greatest blessings. I will always love you unconditionally, no matter where life takes us, and my love for you will never fade. You are the best things that ever happened to me, and I am forever grateful to walk this life with all of you by my side.

Preface

I always wanted to write about my life, finding solace in the therapeutic rhythm of words as I navigate the complexities of my internal battles. This book is not just a recounting of events; it's a beacon of hope for anyone who has felt the crushing weight of not belonging, of never feeling good enough. It's about rising above those feelings, about refusing to let the past dictate our future.

Throughout my journey, I've come to believe in the profound power of divine timing—the moments when we are guided to a person or a place precisely when we need them most. These instances, seemingly orchestrated by a higher order, remind us that we are exactly where we are meant to be, at the precise moment we are meant to be there.

In later chapters of my life, I encountered someone uniquely influential, someone who ignited a transformation within me. Their presence unlocked a floodgate of emotions and words, propelling me to finally put pen to paper and share my story.

This book is a testament to the resilience of the human spirit and the transformative power of connection. It is my sincere hope that by sharing my journey, others may find inspiration to embrace their own path with courage and authenticity.

Six of the Best

"What is it you're looking for today?" Her voice is calm and direct, the question one I've heard often enough that it no longer catches me off guard. There's no judgment in her tone, just steady professionalism as if she's asking about the weather or the time of day.

"A caning session," I reply, my voice steady but weighted. It's not a craving I can always articulate, but it's one that's become part of my rhythm, something deeper than the surface. Today, I want to feel pain—that much I know. It's a strange need, hard to put into words, yet undeniable. A peculiar act of release, one that has worked its way into my bones, a rhythm as familiar as breathing.

I take a sip of water, the cool liquid steadying my hand before I begin the familiar ritual. Standing in the centre of the room, I remove my trousers, the movement deliberate, each action a part of the process. I leave myself clad only in a black T-shirt and matching underwear. The contrast between the everyday simplicity of my clothing and the gravity of what is about to happen strikes me every time. In this moment, the world outside fades, and I become absorbed in the ritual, in its structure. There is comfort in this simplicity, in how it allows me to focus inwardly, to carve out a space just for myself.

As I stand there, the faint chill of the room brushes against my skin, sharpening my senses, drawing me deeper into the moment. The temperature changes the texture of the air, adding a layer of awareness, a heightened alertness to the unfolding scene. Internally, I begin to prepare myself. My thoughts flit between the anticipation of the pain and the focus required to endure it. The duality is always there: the instinct to brace, and the surrender to what's coming. The battle of tension and release.

The bench is prepared, its sturdy frame waiting silently like an old friend offering comfort in its constancy. I lower myself onto it, the smooth surface cool against my bare skin. My body presses into the cool wood, grounding me, making me aware of every inch. I take a quiet, measured breath, letting the air fill my lungs before slowly releasing it. It's a small act of control, a final moment of calm before everything changes. The world holds its breath with me.

The atmosphere shifts as she moves behind me. I hear the subtle, almost faint swish of the cane being tested in the air. The sound is sharp, cutting through the tension, deliberate, as though she is preparing for something important. The weight of it hangs in the air. Her movements are measured, precise—she has done this countless times, and her focus is unwavering. She is not here to be gentle. She is here to deliver what I've asked for.

I close my eyes, letting the anticipation build, the silence between us deepening. There's an odd, almost peaceful stillness in the room, despite the electric undercurrent of what is about to happen. It's a strange mix of trust and tension, knowing that the next moments will bring pain, but also knowing that it is exactly what I need. This is not about cruelty—it is about release, and I am ready.

And then it begins.

The first strike lands with precision, a searing line of fire across my skin. One. The pain is immediate, intense, a sharp sting that radiates outward, flooding my senses before settling into a dull, throbbing pulse. My breath catches for just a moment, a fleeting hesitation, but then I steady myself. This is the moment I've been waiting for. The pain grounds me in a way nothing else can. It's raw, honest, and unforgiving—but it is mine.

Another strike. Two. The sound of the cane slicing through the air is almost as sharp as the impact itself. It cuts the silence with a sharpness that matches the pain. The rhythm is unrelenting, measured yet constant. With each stroke, I feel the layers of tension within me unravelling, dissolving, replaced by something more immediate. The sensation of the present, stripping away the distractions, leaving only what is real.

Three. Four. Five. Six. The numbers blur together, each stroke carving its own distinct mark, both on my body and in my mind. Time becomes irrelevant, lost in the ebb and flow of the pain. It's an intense paradox: painful yet freeing, overwhelming yet clarifying. The sensation builds, like waves crashing, leaving me with an odd sense of peace after each strike, as if each stroke brings me closer to something essential.

As the session continues, I notice the shift. The initial sharpness of each strike begins to evolve. The pain, though still acute, deepens, morphing into something more grounded. It's no longer just physical—it becomes meditative, almost soothing. The external sensations begin to strip away the noise within me, leaving only clarity. The emptiness inside me that has so often screamed for release now feels at peace.

At some point, I realise that my breathing has shifted. What began as shallow gasps has become slow and deliberate, each breath a grounding force. The rhythm of the strikes and the rhythm of my breath begin to merge, intertwining, creating a strange, almost hypnotic harmony. The world falls away until all that is left is the air in my lungs, the beat of my heart, and the steady rhythm of the cane.

When the session ends, I lie still for a moment, letting the echoes of the strikes linger on my skin and in my mind. There's a rawness to it all, but also a profound sense of release, as if a weight has been lifted, even if just for a moment. The pain, intense as it was, has served its purpose. It has cleared the air. I feel lighter, more centred—a strange yet undeniable catharsis.

As I rise from the bench and begin to dress, I glance at her. There's no need for words. Her calm, steady gaze says everything. This ritual, as unconventional as it may be, is ours. And in that silent exchange, I feel understood.

Today, it gave me exactly what I was looking for.

The Great Escape

The sun hung low on the horizon, casting a soft, golden glow over the small yard. The long shadows of the fence stretched lazily across the grass, and the air carried the scent of dust and the faintest hint of a summer evening breeze. I stood at the edge of our worn wooden fence, my fingers brushing against the splintered edges of the posts, a small, tattered backpack slung over my shoulder. Inside it were my most treasured possessions: an old monkey, its fur matted and one eye missing; a sketchbook filled with half-finished drawings; and a few broken crayons. These were my only comforts; the things I carried with me like a shield against the world.

I was only six, but the weight of my thoughts and the intensity of my feelings made me feel older. Quiet, sensitive, and often misunderstood, I was a child who felt things deeply, especially the sharp sting of my mother's words. I often wondered if she even saw me— the real me—or if I was just another source of frustration in her eyes. Her sharp, biting words cut deeper than she probably intended. But to me, they felt like deliberate jabs, each one harder than the last.

Today had been one of those days when everything went wrong, and I was the unfortunate target of her frustration. I couldn't remember what had set her off—whether it was a spilled glass of milk or a misplaced toy—but it didn't matter. The result was always the same. Her anger boiled over, and I felt like I was drowning in the flood of her rage.

"I can't stand the sight of you, Roux!" she had shouted, her voice like a slap. "You're nothing special." The words echoed in my mind, replaying over and over as I stood there, gripping the rough wood of the fence. Her gaze had burned into me, icy and filled with a fury I didn't understand, and her last words—"You always think you're so great, but you're just an ungrateful child"—hung in the air like a sentence I couldn't escape.

I stared at the fence, feeling the urge to run, to leave the pain behind, to find a place where I was loved and understood. In my young mind, it seemed simple. I could just leave, and maybe everything would be better. The fence, weathered and worn, represented the escape I so desperately craved, a way to break free from a world that often felt too cold, too hard.

Just as I was about to hoist myself over the fence, I heard the crunch of gravel under boots, and my heart sank. My father was coming, and he was the last person I wanted to see right now.

"Roux, what are you doing out here?" he called, his voice sharp but tinged with a hint of curiosity.

I froze, fingers still gripping the top of the fence, my small body trembling with a mix of fear and frustration.

"I'm running away," I said, trying to sound more confident than I felt. The words came out a little too loud, as if I could convince both him and myself that I had everything figured out.

He chuckled, but it wasn't a warm sound. It was more of a dry, humourless laugh, the kind that made me feel smaller than I already did.

"Running away? And where exactly do you plan to go?" he asked, his voice a mix of disbelief and judgment.

I hesitated, suddenly aware of how empty my plan was. I didn't have a place to go, not really. I just wanted to escape. "I don't know," I muttered, the boldness draining out of me like sand through my fingers.

He moved closer, his heavy boots crunching the gravel as he knelt to my level. His eyes softened slightly, but there was still an edge to his voice as he spoke. "Roux, you can't just run away every time things get tough. You need to face your problems instead of running from them."

I looked down at the ground, my heart sinking. "But she hates me," I whispered, the words barely escaping my lips. My throat felt tight, and tears pressed at the back of my eyes, threatening to spill over. "I just want to be somewhere I'm loved."

He sighed, and for a moment, I thought he might say something comforting. But instead, his words came out sharp, harder than I expected. "Your mother doesn't hate you, Roux. She's just tired of your nonsense. Running away isn't going to fix anything."

The sting of his words hit me harder than I wanted to admit. I felt smaller than ever, like a child who didn't know how to make things right. Here I was, with food on the table and a roof over my head, and yet I felt ungrateful for wanting more. The weight of it all pressed down on me, making my chest tight.

"Get back inside," he said curtly, standing up and turning toward the house. "We've got enough problems without you causing more."

I followed him, my fingers clenched around the straps of my backpack, the fabric digging into my palms. With each step, the longing for freedom faded, replaced by the heavy reality of staying. A deep ache in my chest, I glanced back at the fence one last time, as if it held the answers I couldn't reach.

Inside, the house felt colder than ever, despite the warmth of the fading sunlight. Fear, sadness, and something else—defiance, maybe—swirled inside me. Maybe things would never get better. Maybe I would always feel like a burden, a mistake too big to fix.

But somewhere deep inside, a spark of determination flickered. One day, I promised myself, I would find a way to be both bold and sensitive, without feeling small. And maybe, just maybe, I would find a place where I was truly loved.

Water Runs Thicker Than Blood

When I was six years old, I found out I was adopted. Decades later, I still remember that moment like it happened yesterday. It's clear in my mind, sharp and vivid like a fresh photograph. That day, everything changed, as if a fog I hadn't noticed before was suddenly gone. In that instant, my life divided into two: the life I thought I knew; and the truth that had always been there, waiting to be uncovered.

The afternoon started like any other, with the soft golden sunlight streaming through the curtains, painting warm streaks across the living room floor. I was lost in my little world of toys; the kind of peaceful play that made time feel like it stood still. The light felt gentle, almost dreamlike. But something in the air was different—subtle, yet impossible to ignore. The familiar sounds of the house—the wind brushing the windows, the faint clatter of dishes—were replaced by an odd stillness, a quiet that felt heavy.

My mother moved through the room with an unease I didn't understand. She wasn't her usual self. Her hands lingered on the laundry basket, hesitating, as though she didn't know what to do next. Her presence was softer, more cautious, as if she were holding onto words too big to say.

When she finally spoke, her voice wasn't the one I knew. It was gentle, careful, almost fragile—so unlike the brisk tone she usually used. It carried a warmth that felt out of place, leaving me confused and uneasy. The carefulness in her words, the way she tiptoed around whatever she was holding back, only deepened the strange weight of the moment. Something was about to change, though I didn't know what.

I was on the floor, clutching a small plastic figure in my hand, its bright colours worn from hours of play. My brother, just a few feet away, was absorbed in his world of toys, his face etched with the concentration only a child could possess. The air between us was peaceful, the quiet hum of childhood innocence filling the room. But then her voice sliced through the calm, unusually calm, and it made us both pause.

She called us over, and we both shuffled closer, the hairs on the back of my neck standing on end, as though we sensed the shift in the atmosphere. Something was different today—something important was about to be revealed.

"You're old enough to understand this now," she began, her voice oddly steady, each word landing with weight. Her hands rested on her lap, fingers twisting slightly, betraying the composure she was trying to project. She looked at us carefully, her gaze lingering between my brother and me, as though she was calculating, measuring the impact of her next words. The room felt suddenly smaller, the air heavier, as if the walls were listening, too.

And then she said it.

"You're adopted," she said finally, her voice soft but steady, each syllable like a stone dropped into a still pond. The words hung in the air, thick and thickening with each passing moment, as my mind struggled to catch up with the meaning they carried.

For a moment, the room seemed to go silent. The words she had spoken echoed in my mind, but they felt too big, too heavy, too strange to fit into my small, six-year-old world. It was as if time itself had paused, holding its breath. My brother and I exchanged glances, both of us too young to fully grasp the weight of what we had just heard, but we could feel the shift in the air, a subtle change that pulled us from the safety of childhood innocence into something we couldn't yet understand.

"What does that mean?" I asked quietly, my voice barely above a whisper, as if speaking any louder might shatter the fragile moment. My fingers tightened around the toy in my hand, the plastic pressing into my palm, but it offered no comfort.

"It means your birth mothers couldn't take care of you," she said, her voice still gentle but carrying an edge of finality. There was something almost clinical in her tone, as if she hoped those few words would be enough to explain everything, to make it all make sense. But they didn't.

I froze, my mind struggling to process what she had just said. The way she delivered the news—soft but detached, as if explaining something routine—left me feeling unmoored, like a boat adrift in a storm without a paddle. Something deep inside me shifted, as though the ground I had been standing on was no longer solid, as though the very foundation of my reality had cracked.

I don't remember much of what happened immediately after that. The world seemed to blur, and I think I went quiet, retreating into the safety of my thoughts. My senses dulled, and I let the silence envelop me, shielding me from the flood of emotions threatening to spill over. But I do remember the storm of emotions that followed: confusion, disbelief, and then a strange, unexpected clarity.

Everything made sense in that moment, as if the pieces of a puzzle that had never quite fit together suddenly clicked into place.

The feeling was difficult to articulate then and still is now. It was as though I had always known, deep down, that something didn't quite fit, like a note in a song that was slightly off-key but no-one could pinpoint why. My family, my life, felt like puzzle pieces forced together, their edges grinding awkwardly instead of clicking into place. Their ways of being, how they spoke, how they acted, how they treated me, always felt foreign, like a language I could mimic but never master.

That day, I knew I was different. The realisation settled in like a shadow, long and undeniable, stretching across the parts of me I hadn't yet learned to understand.

It was like a light had been switched on in a dark room. Suddenly, everything shifted. All the little things that had nagged at me over the years, things I had never quite understood, began to align. My hair didn't look like theirs. My laugh didn't sound like theirs. My interests, the things that sparked excitement in me, seemed like they belonged to someone from a different universe entirely—like artifacts from a world I could observe but never truly understand. And then, the darker thoughts crept in, as insidious as a shadow slowly stretching across the floor.

This must be some kind of mistake, I thought. I wasn't supposed to be here. I couldn't be. Somewhere out there, beyond the walls of this house, was the family I was meant to belong to—the one whose arms I would fit into perfectly; the one where I would feel seen, understood, and accepted for exactly who I was. I felt a deep ache, a longing I couldn't put into words, that one day they would come for me, that one day everything would be made right.

For years after that, the realisation shaped everything about how I viewed the world and my place in it. It became the lens through which I processed every experience, every interaction, every hurt. I began to notice the small but sharp ways my mother treated me differently from how she treated others. The coldness in her voice, the quick snap of her temper, the almost subtle distance in her gaze. It wasn't apparent enough for anyone else to notice, but I felt it deeply—like a weight in the room that no-one else could see but that I was burdened with every day.

When she scolded me or brushed me off, I'd remind myself of one thing that, strangely, gave me a kind of comfort: I didn't carry her DNA. I wasn't *really* hers.

It became a mantra I clung to, especially in my darkest moments.

You're not like them. You're not one of them.

At first, that thought brought me a small sense of relief, like a cool breeze after suffocating heat. But it also came with an unbearable weight: the feeling of being stuck. Because while I could dream of another life, of another family that would love me the way I longed to be loved, I was still here. I was still theirs. I couldn't escape.

The only way I knew how to cope was to escape into my imagination. It was the only place where I could create a world where I was more than the misplaced child who didn't fit in.

I spent countless days dreaming of being saved, playing out elaborate scenes in my mind where my real mother would finally come for me. In these fantasies, she was beautiful and kind, with soft eyes that held all the love I had been missing. She'd sweep me up in her arms and tell me how sorry she was for leaving me, how much she had missed me, how she had been searching for me all this time.

"I'm here now," she'd say. "You're safe."

Sometimes, I'd pretend I could hear her voice calling out to me, whispering promises of a better life. I'd imagine her face, though it was always blurry, a collage of features I must have seen on strangers or in books. In my dreams, she was everything I needed her to be: warm, gentle, perfect.

But she never came for me.

The weight of that truth settled in slowly over the years, like a heavy stone pressing down on my chest. No matter how many times I replayed those imaginary reunions, I always woke up in the same place: the small, suffocating world I was trying so hard to escape.

And yet, I couldn't stop dreaming.

Even as I grew older, the fantasy lingered. It became less about being rescued and more about finding answers. Who was she? Why had she given me up? Did she think of me? Did she miss me?

These questions haunted me, shaping my relationships, my decisions, my sense of self. I started to view everything through the perspective of abandonment and belonging. Every rejection, no matter how small, felt like a confirmation of what I had always feared: that I wasn't wanted. That I wasn't enough.

But at the same time, I held onto a stubborn hope that somewhere out there, someone was missing me, too. Someone was thinking of me, wondering where I was, longing to find me just as much as I longed to find them.

Looking back now, I realise how much that moment at six years old defined me. It was the day I began to question everything—the people who raised me, the world around me, and myself. It was the day I learned that the truth could be both a gift and a burden.

In some ways, it gave me strength. It taught me how to dream, how to hold onto hope even when reality felt unbearable. But it also left scars, wounds that I'm still learning how to heal.

I don't know if I'll ever find all the answers I'm looking for, or if the woman I dreamed about as a child even exists in the way I imagined her. But I do know this: the little girl I was, the one who learned at six years old that her world wasn't what she thought it was, deserved love. She deserved kindness. She deserved to feel like she belonged.

A Life on Edge

The room is a patchwork of shadows and faint light. The soft orange glow from the streetlamp outside spills through the gap in the curtains, casting jagged shapes onto the walls, like fractured memories waiting to be pieced together. I sit on my bed, knees pulled up to my chest, my arms wrapped tightly around Monkey. He isn't just a toy. He is my sanctuary; my only constant in a world that shifts unpredictably around me. His fur, once fluffy and a rich chocolate brown, is now dull and matted, worn thin in patches. His button eyes, scratched and dulled, still shine in my eyes like tiny stars—warm, knowing, never judgmental.

I press my cheek against his head, the fabric worn soft from years of being clutched and cried into. My tears soak into his fur, and Monkey, as always, absorbs them silently, a quiet witness to the storm I carry inside. I whisper into the stillness of the room, my voice shaky but soft, barely rising above the low hum of the heater, like the faint echo of my heartache.

"Why does she hate me so much, Monkey?" My fingers tighten around his tiny arms, the motion grounding me, as if holding him closer will stop my voice from breaking. "I try to be good. I try so hard. But nothing is ever enough."

The air feels heavy and oppressive, as though my words have weight and are filling every corner of the room, pushing everything else aside. My mother's fury from earlier lingers like a sour taste—sharp, cutting, lingering in my mouth long after the words have been spoken. Every word she spat at me still rings in my ears, each glare and hiss replaying vividly in my mind, relentless, refusing to let me rest. I try to push it all down, to bury it deep, but the echoes are persistent, gnawing at my thoughts.

"You know what she said today, don't you?" My voice drops lower, as if I'm afraid someone might hear. "She said I was stealing. But I wasn't, Monkey. I wasn't." The memory twists inside me, hot and suffocating. My voice cracks as more tears spill over, trailing down my cheeks, and Monkey takes it all in, steadfast and unyielding, as though absorbing my pain is his only purpose.

I hug him tighter, burying my face in his familiar scent— one part fabric softener, one part something uniquely his. It comforts me, even though I know it doesn't change anything. "Why doesn't she believe me? Why does she always think I'm lying?" The question drifts into the air, unanswered but insistent, like a question without an end, a riddle that my small heart cannot solve.

I shift on the bed, curling my body around Monkey as though I can shield him from the storm that rages inside me. The day replays in my mind, vivid and unrelenting, each moment etched into my memory like a scar. My mother's hand gripping my wrist, her sharp tug as she dragged me through the school gates. The humiliation of standing in front of my classmates while she demanded I apologise for "stealing" the chalk my teacher had given me. My teacher tried to explain, tried to intervene, but my mother didn't care. The truth didn't matter.

"I told her the truth," I whisper, my voice thick with emotion. "But she didn't care. She never cares." My mother's words slice through my memory like a razor: *You're a liar.* But it's not just the words; it's the look in her eyes, the disgust in her voice, the way she saw me as something less than human. That is what hurts the most—the way she looks at me like I am something dirty, something unworthy.

I wipe my nose on my sleeve, a small rebellion I relish even here, in the safety of my room. She hates it when I do that, but Monkey doesn't mind. Monkey never minds. He's the only one who listens.

"You're the only one who understands," I tell him, my voice trembling, like a fragile leaf in a storm. "Dad doesn't see it. He's never here enough to see it." My fingers trace the worn edges of Monkey's ear, a habit that soothes me, that makes me feel like I'm not completely lost. "And even if he did, he wouldn't do anything. He tried once, remember? He told her to be nicer. And you saw what happened after that."

The memory surges forward, sharp and visceral. My father, sitting at the dining table with his newspaper, his brow furrowing as I haltingly told him about her sharp words and impossible punishments. He had listened—or at least seemed to. He had promised to talk to her, and for a moment, I dared to hope that things might change.

But the next morning, her fury was like a hurricane—loud, unrelenting, and terrifying. She cornered me in the kitchen, her voice low and venomous as she hissed, *"Don't you ever talk about me again. You think I'm hard on you now! Just wait. I'll make your life a living hell if you open that mouth of yours again."*

My heart races just thinking about it. I hug Monkey closer, trying to steady myself. I haven't dared to confide in my father since. The risk is too great.

"I wish I could run away," I murmur into Monkey's ear. "Take you with me and go somewhere far, far away. Somewhere she can't find me." The thought is both terrifying and intoxicating. I don't know where I would go, don't know if the world outside this house would be any kinder, but the idea of escaping—of leaving this place and this life behind—feels like a flicker of light in an otherwise endless darkness.

I shift again, tucking Monkey against my chest. His small frame fits perfectly against me, his worn fur soft beneath my fingers. I stroke the threadbare patch on his arm, the one I love most—the one that's been stitched and restitched so many times it no longer matches the rest of him. That patch is proof that he's endured, that he's survived. Just like me.

"Do you think I'll ever get out of here, Monkey?" I ask, my voice small, like a whisper in the dark. "Do you think things will ever get better?"

He doesn't answer, of course. But in my mind, I imagine his voice, gentle and steady, full of the reassurance I crave. *"You're strong, Roux,"* I hear him say. *"Stronger than you think. You'll get through this. I promise."*

I know the words are my own, but in Monkey's voice, they feel real. They feel like hope.

The night stretches on, the house is silent and still around me. My thoughts flit between the pain of today and the fragile dreams of tomorrow. I imagine a life beyond this one, a life where I don't have to scan her face for danger, where I can laugh without fear, where I can just be. I imagine a place where I don't feel so small, where I can stretch my arms wide and breathe without suffocating.

"When I grow up," I whisper, my voice filled with quiet determination, "I'll be different. I'll be kind. I'll listen. I'll never make anyone feel the way she makes me feel."

It's a promise, both to myself and to Monkey. It's a vow to break the cycle, to become the person I wish she could be, but can't seem to be.

The shadows on the wall stretch as the hours pass, their shapes changing with the soft movement of the streetlamp outside. I lie down, tucking Monkey under my chin, my fingers tracing the edge of his ear in a motion that calms me even as my thoughts swirl.

"Thank you, Monkey," I whisper, my voice barely audible now, the weight of everything pressing down. "For everything."

Sink or Swim

The world feels enormous when you're small, and my hand is barely big enough to grip my mother's as she leads me up the gravel driveway. The crunch of the pebbles beneath our feet echoes in the quiet afternoon, a sound that seems too loud against the heavy silence that surrounds us. In front of us stands a large house, towering and imposing, its sheer size making everything around it feel smaller, less significant. It has the kind of beauty that feels distant, unreachable—like something out of a storybook, but not the kind of place where you're invited to play.

The lawn is perfectly manicured, each blade of grass standing to attention, a lush carpet of green stretching out in all directions, the meticulousness almost unnatural. High fences surround the property, dark wooden slats reaching up toward the sky, their height making me feel small and insignificant—like I am a child standing at the gate of something grand and untouchable.

I can feel the tension in my chest growing tighter with each step, though I don't yet fully understand why. My mom has been talking about swimming lessons for weeks, but it's only now, standing at the threshold of the house, that it feels real. Something I can't escape. Something big.

I glance up at her face. She's smiling, but it's forced—a fragile thing, as if she's trying to reassure me and maybe herself. But her eyes—her eyes tell a different story. They're full of uncertainty, shadowed by something I can't quite name, and I can't help but wonder if she's as nervous as I am. I feel a pang of guilt, not knowing if it's right to be scared, but somehow understanding that she might be feeling the same way.

When we knock on the door, it swings open almost immediately, as if the woman inside had been waiting for us, listening for our arrival. The door creaks on its hinges, and there she is, standing in the threshold—a towering figure who seems as much a part of the house as the stone walls and the iron gate. She looks like someone who could snap a tree in half if she wanted to, her broad shoulders and thick, muscular arms giving the impression of raw strength. Her hair is pulled back in a tight bun, not a strand out of place, and her eyes are hard, unreadable. There's no softness in her gaze—only the kind of steely resolve that makes it clear she's not here to coddle anyone, not here to make me feel safe.

"Come on in," she says, her voice low and gravelly, carrying an unspoken command, a quiet force that seems to make the air itself hold its breath. It's the kind of voice that could shake the ground beneath us, and I feel it reverberate through my bones.

My mom nods quickly, and still holding her hand, I step forward cautiously, trying to hide behind her, as if her presence could shield me from the woman's gaze. But it's no use. Her eyes lock onto mine, sharp and unwavering, and she doesn't smile. She doesn't need to.

Her very presence is enough to make me feel small, like I'm just another task on her list that she's going to handle with cold efficiency.

She leads the way outside to the pool, walking steadily, her steps sure and calm. We follow quietly behind her, the only sound coming from our footsteps and the soft rustling of leaves in the breeze. The air is warm, with a faint hint of chlorine mixed with the smell of nearby flowers. The pool comes into view, its surface still and reflective, shining under the open sky.

Without a word, she steps forward, her large hands reaching out to lift me effortlessly off the ground. I let out a small yelp of surprise, the air rushing from my chest. But before I can even fully comprehend what's happening, she throws me into the air. Time seems to stretch as I fall, weightless for just a moment, before the cold, unyielding water crashes around me. The world goes dark, muffled, as I sink below the surface. My limbs flail, panic surging through me as I try to find the air, my heart hammering in my chest. I can hear my mom shouting from the edge of the pool, but her voice sounds distant, like it's underwater too, a blur of noise I can't quite reach.

I kick and struggle, my body moving without direction, my mind frozen in a chaotic blur. I can't breathe. I'm sinking deeper. What just happened? Why am I in here? The water is thick, swallowing me whole, and my thoughts are a swirl of confusion. But then I hear it— her voice, sharp and clear above the chaos. *"She'll make it to the edge."*

Her words slice through the panic, cutting through the fog of fear and grounding me, somehow. I don't fully understand them, but something in me shifts. It's like a switch has been flipped. A deep, instinctive knowing takes over. I don't know where it comes from, but it's there, solid and unshakable. I can do this.

I push my arms through the water and kick my legs hard, fighting against the weight of the water that feels like it's trying to pull me down. My little body protests, muscles screaming, but I keep going, the edge just within reach. I can make it. I have to.

And then, by some miracle, my fingers brush against the rough concrete of the pool's edge. I grab it with all my strength, pulling myself out of the water, my breath coming in desperate, shaky gasps. My mom is there, standing at the side of the pool, her face pale and tight with anxiety. She looks like she's been holding her breath the whole time, like she's just exhaled for the first time since I fell in. I catch my own breath, still trembling, my body cold and slick with water, but there's a strange warmth spreading inside me too. I feel stronger now. I did it. I made it.

That lesson would stay with me forever. Throughout my life, I would find myself thrown into situations that felt just as overwhelming, just as impossible. But no matter how deep the water, no matter how far the edge seemed, I would always find a way to swim. The lessons that woman taught me with her stern presence and few words would carry me through, because I knew, deep down, that I would always make it to the edge.

The Game

The rhythmic thud-thud-thud of the tennis ball against the wall carries a steady beat, grounding me in a way few things can. I stand in the backyard, gripping my old wooden racket tightly, its weight familiar in my small hands. The strings are loose, threatening to snap with each strike. The grip is worn smooth, and the wood underneath is exposed in places, the marks of years spent in my hands. The frame bears dents and scratches from countless hours of use, but I don't mind. It's mine, or at least I tell myself it is, even though I found it buried in the attic among forgotten boxes—a relic from another time.

The wall is my opponent, silent but unwavering, never judging, never shouting. Hour after hour, I hit the ball against the brick, each bounce and return stroke a little victory. The racket vibrates slightly with each hit, the sensation grounding me as I lose myself in the rhythm. The ball comes back fast, then slow, then at a wild angle, but I adjust each time, finding the right spot on the racket, the perfect swing to send it back. With each stroke, the tension in my body eases, replaced by the quiet hum of concentration.

I picture myself on a real court, with real players. In my mind, the wall transforms into an opponent, skilled but not unbeatable. The sound of the ball echoes louder in my imagination, blending with the roar of a cheering crowd. I see myself diving for impossible shots, delivering perfect serves, and winning points against the best. I have no coach, no lessons, and none of the shiny equipment the kids at school brag about, but I don't need them. Not here, not in my backyard with my racket and my wall. In these moments, it's enough.

*

The memory of that tournament still feels vivid, like an oasis in the desert of my childhood. It had started with a flyer tacked to the bulletin board at school: *Open Junior Tennis Tournament, Ages 8-12*. My heart skipped a beat when I read it. A tournament. An actual tournament. For days, I couldn't think about anything else. It was like a dream I could almost touch.

I raced home that afternoon, my mind already filled with images of myself on the court, the sound of the crowd cheering, the thrill of hitting the winning shot. I burst through the door, nearly tripping over the rug in my haste, and blurted it out before I could lose my nerve.

"I'm going to play in a tennis tournament!"

My mother barely glanced up from the glossy magazine she was flipping through. Her nails clicked against the page as she turned it, her disinterest obvious. "A tennis tournament? What's the point? You'll lose interest in five minutes, just like you do with everything else."

Her words hit me like a gut punch, a weight sinking into my chest. But I refused to back down. "But I practise every day!" I gripped the old wooden racket in my hand so tightly my fingers ached. "I want to play in this. I'll do well, I promise!"

My father, sitting across the room with a newspaper spread in his lap, barely looked up. "You've got that racket, don't you? Use that. Kids these days don't appreciate what they have."

"It's old," I said, my voice wavering as I held up the battered relic. "It's... broken."

"Well, borrow one," my mother said with a dismissive wave. "We're not wasting money on something you'll quit next week."

I stood there for a moment, my excitement deflated, but I refused to let their words stop me. That night, I called my friend Lily, who had a sleek, shiny racket she barely used. She didn't hesitate when I asked if I could borrow it.

"Of course," she said, as if it were the easiest thing in the world.

When she handed it to me the next day, it felt like holding a piece of magic. It was light and smooth, the grip perfectly moulded to my hand. For the first time, I felt like I might actually stand a chance.

The morning of the tournament felt suffocating, the heat oppressive even before the sun climbed fully into the sky. The courts were a fiery red, shimmering with the morning's warmth, and I stepped onto them barefoot. My sneakers had given up weeks ago, the soles cracked and flapped, and my parents hadn't replaced them yet. My toes curled against the warm, abrasive sand as I took my place near the registration desk, clutching the borrowed racket like it was a lifeline.

The eyes of the other players and their parents followed me, quiet whispers threading through the air like strands of unease. My mismatched clothes—shorts that didn't quite fit, and an oversized T-shirt—made me stand out in stark contrast to their crisp, coordinated outfits. The borrowed racket gleamed, pristine in my hands, almost mocking my rough appearance.

But I didn't care. Not about the whispers, the glances, or the unspoken judgment. I didn't come here for them. I didn't come here for my parents either, who couldn't be bothered to show up. I came for myself, to see what I could do, to test the hours spent hitting against a silent wall in my backyard.

The first match began under a blazing sun that felt like it was pressing down on my shoulders. The heat was unrelenting, sweat trickling down my forehead and stinging my eyes. My opponent's strokes were sharp and practised, but I met every volley with focus and determination. The borrowed racket felt strange at first, its lighter frame throwing off my rhythm, but I adjusted quickly. My strokes grew steadier, my movements more deliberate. I lost track of time, my entire world narrowing to the ball, the racket, the court.

When I won the first match, a surge of pride bloomed in my chest. I shook my opponent's hand and glanced toward the sidelines, half-expecting to see my parents there. Of course, they weren't.

The second match was tougher. My opponent was faster, her movements fluid and sharp. Each point was a battle, my feet digging into the red clay as I sprinted for the ball, my muscles straining with every return. By the end of the match, I was drenched in sweat, my T-shirt sticking to my back like a second skin, but I won. Another round conquered.

By the time I reached the semi-finals, the heat had become unbearable. My bare feet burned with every step, the rough sand grinding against my skin, but I forced myself to keep going. I fought through each point, ignoring the sharp sting of blisters forming on my heels and the balls of my feet. The pain was a constant, nagging presence, but I shoved it to the back of my mind. I was so close.

"Just one more set," I whispered to myself between breaths. "Just one more game."

The semi-final was the hardest yet. My opponent was relentless, and every point felt like a test of endurance. My feet ached, and the blisters throbbed with each pivot and sprint, but I kept pushing. When I finally won the last point, I dropped to my knees, exhausted but exhilarated. I was going to the finals.

As I stood up, brushing the sand off my legs, I noticed the looks of the other players and the parents on the sidelines. Their expressions had changed, no longer pitying or dismissive. There was something else now: respect. I felt it in their nods, their quiet conversations as I passed by. For the first time, I felt like I'd proven myself.

But the final was a different story. By then, my feet were a mess of torn skin and raw flesh, the blisters had burst and left open wounds that bled into the red sand. Every step sent a jolt of agony up my legs, and my movements became sluggish and uncoordinated. My strokes, once sharp and precise, grew sloppy. I saw the frustration in my opponent's eyes turn to pity as she won point after point with ease.

I tried to ignore the pain, to focus on the ball, but my body betrayed me. My legs felt like lead, my vision blurred from the heat and exhaustion, and the racket grew heavy in my hands. The match ended quickly, my mistakes piling up until there was no coming back. The polite applause from the crowd stung more than my battered feet.

I sat on the edge of the court, wrapping my arms around my knees as the final winner was crowned. My chest felt hollow, and my heart sank with the weight of defeat. I had fought so hard and pushed myself to the very edge, but it hadn't been enough. I had wanted to prove that I was worthy of lessons, of a proper racket, of shoes. And yet, here I was, barefoot, bloodied, and empty-handed.

The walk home stretched endlessly before me, over five kilometres of rough pavement that tore at my already raw feet. Each step was agony, the sting of grit grinding into my wounds with every movement. I kept my head down, clutching the borrowed racket tightly, the only part of this day that felt like a victory.

When I finally reached home, the house was quiet. The faint hum of the TV drifted from the living room, where my brother was sprawled on the couch, absorbed in a show. My parents were nowhere in sight. No-one was waiting to ask how I did; no-one was there to celebrate my small victories or console me for my loss.

I stepped inside, my feet leaving faint streaks of blood on the cool tiles and made my way to the bathroom. I didn't cry. I didn't call out for help. I didn't even allow myself to feel the anger bubbling beneath the surface. Instead, I turned on the faucet and carefully washed the blood and sand from my feet. The water stung, and I bit my lip to keep from gasping, my hands trembling as I cleaned the wounds.

There were no bandages in the house, so I wrapped my feet in paper towels and limped to my room. I set the borrowed racket on my desk, running a damp cloth over the handle to clean off the sweat and dirt. Lily had trusted me with it, and I wanted to return it in the same pristine condition she had given it to me.

Dinner that night was uneventful. I sat at the table, quietly eating while my brother chattered about something he had seen on TV. My parents barely acknowledged me, too absorbed in their own conversation to notice the way I winced with every step or the stiffness in my posture. I didn't offer any details about the tournament and didn't mention the semi-finals, the blisters, or the final round. I ate quickly and retreated to my room.

As I lay in the darkness, my feet throbbing beneath the covers, I replayed the day in my mind. I thought of the matches I had won, the way the crowd watched me with newfound respect, the way I fought through the pain. Despite the final loss, I realised something important:

I had proven myself, not to my parents, not to the other players or their families, but to me.

I had given everything I had and pushed myself beyond what I thought I could endure, and that was something no-one could take away from me. As I closed my eyes, the ache in my body faded into a quiet sense of pride. I had fought. And that was enough.

The Beach

We were on holiday in Scottburgh, South Africa, where the beach stretched out like an endless ribbon of sand, dotted with little rockpools that seemed to hold whole worlds of their own. I spent hours in those pools, lost in my little adventures. The water was clear, shimmering in the sunlight, and I could see crabs scuttling under the rocks, their tiny legs moving frantically, and seaweed swaying lazily in the gentle waves. I loved it there, the sound of the ocean filling my ears, the salt on my skin, lost in a world that was entirely mine.

I was hopping between the pools, jumping from one rock to another, when the current changed. It was sudden and strong, the kind of pull that caught you off-guard, like the sea itself decided to reach out and grab me. One moment, I was standing on solid rock, the sharp edges of the stones cool under my feet; the next, I was being yanked into deeper water.

The force of it stole the air from my lungs, and before I knew it, I was flailing in the current. I screamed for help—loud and desperate, my voice bouncing off the rocks—but it felt like my cries dissolved into the air. No-one seemed to hear me. My aunt was nearby, but she didn't look over. Maybe she thought I was just playing, just another game in the water. Everyone else seemed too absorbed in their world to notice the sea pulling me in, inch by inch, as if it had plans for me that I didn't understand.

Panic clawed at me, my small body fighting against the relentless force of the water. But then, something shifted inside me. A strange calmness filled me as the waves tugged me farther out, carrying me further from the shore. Without thinking, I just floated. I didn't struggle. It was as though the fight had left me in that instant, replaced by an understanding I couldn't explain. Something inside me told me that fighting wouldn't help.

So, I lay there, suspended in the water, my small body bobbing with the rhythm of the waves. It was as though I was being carried by something invisible, steady, like the sea itself was holding me, guiding me.

In that moment, I felt an overwhelming sense of awareness, as if I was no longer just a small child, but someone who was part of this vast, untouchable ocean. Maybe it was the water, or maybe it was something more, something that tied me to the world in ways I hadn't yet understood. I felt a strange sense of safety, as though, no matter what, I wasn't truly alone. Even though I was drifting away, there was something, somewhere, keeping me afloat. It was as if the sea, in its infinite wisdom, knew I would find my way.

But there was something else—something more visceral—that gnawed at my insides. The injustice of it all, the way no-one seemed to care, the way my cries went unheard, burned inside me like a bitter ember. I could see my aunt and cousins standing on the shore, laughing, talking, not even turning their heads. I was there, struggling to stay above water, and yet I felt invisible. *Why doesn't anyone care?* I thought. *Why is no-one paying attention?*

That was when the raw truth hit me, deep and unrelenting: I was close to an ending, and no-one even noticed. It wasn't the water that scared me most—it was the quiet indifference. The crushing realisation that no-one was going to save me but me. I was alone in that vastness, and it would be up to me to make it back.

At that moment, I understood something essential: I had to rely on myself. The world could look away, and the people I trusted could turn their backs, but I had no choice but to trust that floating—just surviving—would be enough.

And then, the current released me. Slowly, the water pushed me back toward the shore. My muscles, exhausted and trembling, fought to keep me afloat as I paddled weakly, but with determination. I finally staggered out of the water, my heart pounding in my chest, my hands shaking. I looked up at my aunt, still talking to my cousins, still unaware of what had just happened. I felt a cold wave of isolation wash over me, but beneath that was a strange, simmering sense of something else.

I learned something important in those few moments. I learned that when the world feels like it's going to swallow you whole, when no-one seems to notice you're sinking, you can only rely on yourself. No-one else is going to pull you out. There's no-one else who can save you. It's always going to be you—floating, fighting, finding your way to the shore, no matter how distant or invisible that shore seems.

As I stood there, dripping wet, the waves lapping against my legs, I realised that I was stronger than I'd ever known. Not because I had been rescued, but because I had saved myself.

The Quiet Pulse of Existence

My childhood was, in many ways, quite ordinary. I spent a lot of time alone, often drawing, reading, or writing—activities that offered me both solace and escape. Reading, in particular, became a refuge—a way to lose myself in the fantasy of a story, to slip into a world where everything was structured, where things made sense.

I was a deeply introspective child, always in my head, quietly observing the world around me. It often felt like I wasn't quite like the others, sensing that I had an unusual ability to read people and situations with an ease that I couldn't explain. I could feel the weight of a room's atmosphere and the unspoken tensions in conversations, and I was acutely aware of the energy around me, especially in others. For a long time, I attributed this heightened sensitivity to my mother's tendency to keep me on edge, but as I grew older, I realised I was an empath. It was only much later in life that I began to understand what that truly meant—the way I absorbed not only people's emotions but the environment around me.

Growing up, I was always labelled as the black sheep of the family. Someone once said something that stayed with me: *"The person who is the black sheep is often the most sensitive, the one who absorbs all the energy of the other family members."* That description resonated deeply within me, especially in our home, which was often full of negative energy. It wasn't the kind of energy that could be easily ignored—it clung to everything. Even during the rare quiet periods, when there was no shouting or fighting, I would retreat to my room, longing for solitude, for peace. Those moments of calm felt like brief respites from the tension in the air, but I always yearned for more. I longed to be left alone, to rest, heal, and not think. The pressure to exist in such a volatile environment took its toll.

Despite my challenging relationship with my mother, some moments felt like glimpses of something resembling a normal mother-daughter bond. She was an exceptional seamstress, a master of her craft, and I would sit for hours beside her, watching as she worked, absorbed in the rhythm of her hands moving across the fabric. The way she figured out what to make, how to cut the material just right, and how she sewed with such precision—it was almost meditative to watch. I would often find myself sorting buttons, rearranging patterns, or tidying up as she went along, finding small ways to participate, to be part of her world.

Threading the sewing machine was always my favourite part—a simple task, but one that gave me a sense of pride. Even as an adult, I could still do it with my eyes closed. She sewed constantly—for herself, for us, and for others who needed custom pieces. Though I wasn't a fan of wearing homemade clothes, those quiet moments with her, surrounded by the hum of the sewing machine, felt like rare windows into a more conventional, perhaps even idealised, mother-daughter relationship—fleeting but meaningful in their simplicity.

In our household, helping with meals and cleaning up was an expectation, particularly for me. I despised the dated, traditional view of a woman's role in the home. While the men had the freedom to do as they pleased, the women bore the burden of everything else. This bred a sense of resentment in me. I wasn't the kind of girl who wanted to conform to a world shaped by those expectations.

I often wondered if this resentment stemmed from the forced traditions, the absence of a strong male role model, or perhaps from the fact that my biological father had left like a coward. That sense of abandonment always made me view women as the stronger of the two genders, so taking on a weaker role was something I disliked intensely.

Sundays were the worst for me. The day began early, with my mother preparing lunch before church. Cooking seemed to take hours as we prepped the meat, vegetables, and dessert, only to rush off to church and Sunday school. Sundays became a ritual of monotony from my earliest memories. I wished we could spend the day differently—hiking, biking, or meeting friends—but Sundays were a holy day of misery.

After church, we would return home to finish preparing lunch. Eating together wasn't a joyous or social occasion. Instead, it was often done in silence, the mood entirely dependent on whether my parents had argued that morning. Afterwards, my brother and I were responsible for washing the dishes, a task we loathed but never dared to complain about. We had a dishwasher but never used it—something I still find baffling.

The rest of Sunday was like a funeral procession. The house felt steeped in boredom and suffocating silence, with everyone keeping to themselves. The stillness of the afternoon weighed on me, heavy and oppressive. I would retreat to my room, a space of small escape, but even there, I couldn't escape the thick, unspoken tension that lingered in every corner of the house. I longed for Monday to come, to break free from the chains of another Sunday and slip back into the rhythm of school, where there was movement, noise, and a sense of purpose.

Despite the oppressive atmosphere, my brother and I shared many adventures, which provided a much-needed escape. We got into all kinds of mischief—climbing trees, sneaking into abandoned places, and exploring the woods behind the house. We always carried a selection of hunting knives on our adventures, as if to prepare for whatever dangers we imagined might come our way. The weight of the knives in our hands was both comforting and thrilling, a small but fierce symbol of our shared rebellion.

We had an unspoken pact to never reveal our exact whereabouts or the full extent of our escapades, and in those moments of shared secrecy, I found a connection with my brother that was a relief from the loneliness of the rest of the day. It was an adventure that allowed us to momentarily forget the weight of Sundays and the silence that stretched out around us at home.

One day, we decided to explore on our bikes. Life felt different back then—less constrained by the awareness of potential dangers. There was a sense of freedom in the air, a sense that we could conquer anything, no matter how risky or reckless it seemed. We crossed the Klip River, a notoriously dangerous river that flowed through Ladysmith, its waters often rising to flood the town. It was a place we had been warned about, but that only added to the thrill.

As we pedalled across the shallow part of the river, my brother nearly lost his bike to the current. The water surged around his tyres with a force I hadn't fully understood until that moment. How we managed to retrieve the bike without falling in remains a mystery. The river's powerful flow would have been impossible to survive, and yet, somehow, we were lucky that day. The adrenaline rushed through me, making every other danger seem trivial in comparison.

By the time we realised it was dark, we knew we'd be in trouble when we returned home. Still, despite the growing unease in my chest, we didn't hurry. But somehow, my parents found us. They didn't need to say much—just their angry voices calling us back was enough to freeze us in place. When we arrived, my father was standing at the door, cane in hand. He was a tall, imposing figure, and in that moment, I could feel the weight of every punishment he'd ever given us.

The hiding we received that night is burned into my memory, the pain a sharp, searing reminder of that adventure we would never forget. It was a painful end to a day that had been nothing but thrilling—an adventure that, despite the consequences, I wouldn't trade for anything.

I recall another time when my brother and I went to the playground with our maid, Sarafina. For some reason, my mother couldn't take us that day, but I didn't mind. In her absence, we felt a strange, unspoken freedom, as if the usual rules had been lifted. We often tested the limits when our parents weren't around, and that day Sarafina bore the brunt of our mischief.

My brother stumbled across a box of matches, and it was as though we instantly understood that we shouldn't be holding them. The risk, the thrill of it, seemed so alluring, and before we knew it, we were playing with them, daring each other to strike the match and light it in one swift motion. The summer heat hung heavy around us, oppressive, the air thick with the scent of dry earth and brittle grass, evidence of the ongoing drought that had dried everything in sight.

And then, in a heartbeat, it happened. A tiny spark caught, and within seconds, flames tore through the dry field, spreading faster than we could comprehend. We froze, rooted to the spot, too terrified to move as the fire quickly grew out of control. The crackling of the flames was deafening, and the heat radiated off the fire as if the earth itself was burning. People nearby started running, frantic, trying to stop it, but it was futile; the damage was done. The fire roared through the field, unstoppable, and we were left standing there, watching in shock, powerless against the force we had unleashed.

Panicked, we fled the scene, consumed not only by fear of the fire's consequences but by the terror of what would happen if our mother ever found out. The thought of her discovering our recklessness made my heart race, and the shame gnawed at my insides. Sarafina never told on us. Perhaps she was too frightened of what might happen to us—or even to herself—if our mother found out the truth. To this day, I remember her silence as a quiet act of protection, shielding us from the storm that would have followed.

The Realm of Untainted Joy

Growing up, my memories with my mom were few and far between, but those rare moments were unforgettable. One of the highlights was when I'd tag along with her to visit Elsa—a much older woman who owned several businesses, enjoyed hunting, a stiff whiskey, and spoke her mind without hesitation. Elsa's house, almost like a mansion, was enormous, with a pool glistening in the backyard and an outdoor Lapa. In this covered entertainment area, laughter and conversation would always fill the air. Inside, the house felt like a museum of stories, its walls adorned with mounted animal heads, each telling its tale. The tiled floors were covered in thick animal skins, lending the space a rustic, earthy aroma—rich, leathery, and warm. It reminded me of an indoor savanna, where the wildness of nature was tamed yet still very much alive.

The garage was perpetually hung with biltong—the dried, cured meat that is a staple in South African kitchens. Its sharp, savoury smell would fill the air, and I'd always feel a sense of privilege as Elsa waved me over to help myself to any piece I wanted. It was a small freedom I relished. Elsa also had an African grey parrot she adored like a child. The bird could talk, even swear—a fact that, as a child, I found endlessly amusing.

It would mimic Elsa's deep voice, adding an unpredictable edge to the atmosphere, like living comic relief amid all the adult conversation. At one point, she even had a small deer that roamed freely through the house and garden—an irony I found amusing, given the hunting trophies mounted on the walls. The paradox made me smile, though I never mentioned it.

I loved these visits, always filled with interesting happenings and fascinating stories. Elsa and my mom would speak openly in front of me about life— about men, relationships, and other topics that seemed far beyond my age. Their conversations were brutally honest, full of colourful language, often punctuated by one of them turning to me with a mischievous smile and saying, "Close your ears for this one." I never minded—in fact, I loved listening. They struck me as strong women, ones who had lived through countless experiences and possessed the wisdom to speak their truth without hesitation. There was a rawness to their words that captivated me, a confidence I deeply admired.

My mom had another friend, Judy—another entrepreneur we visited from time to time. Like my mom, Judy was a no-nonsense woman, sharp as a tack, and approached life with clear logic and simplicity. I couldn't help but admire her, too. There was something magnetic about these powerful women—the way they moved through the world with such confidence, speaking their minds without hesitation. They didn't care who they offended, yet they exuded an air of calm self-assurance, making their strength even more striking.

It was as if they radiated undeniable power and purpose, leaving an impression on everyone they encountered.

I never quite got the sense that Judy was the maternal type, despite having three children of her own. There was always a certain distance between her and me, a coolness that made me wonder if she found my presence unnecessary or if she simply didn't know how to connect with me. But I was adaptable. I could read the room well and quickly learned that in situations like these it was best to pretend I was engrossed in a book. I'd sit quietly, eyes focused on the pages, while in reality I was fully absorbed in their conversations. Every word they spoke—about life, work, or the world around them—seeped into me, and I soaked it all in like a sponge.

Most of our visits to Judy revolved around planning the annual fundraising event for the child welfare organisation where my mom worked as a secretary. My mom was deeply involved in organising the event, and I loved everything about it—the energy, the buzz, and the feeling of contributing to something bigger. It was exhilarating. The weekend of the event was always intense. We worked tirelessly, setting up, managing details, and attending to every small task. It was exhausting but in the best possible way. There was satisfaction in the hard work and a sense of pride in what we accomplished as the event came together. I thrived on the purpose it gave me, and the exhaustion that followed felt like a badge of honour. Each night, I'd fall into bed, sore and tired, but my heart would be full.

It was also thanks to Judy that I eventually found myself in America later in life. I remember the conversation vividly how Judy, with her straightforward manner and sharp mind, made the connection that set things in motion. She had a way of seeing possibilities where others saw none and of pushing things forward with quiet determination. That was her strength, her influence, and I felt fortunate to have crossed paths with her. Her support acted as a catalyst, leading to an opportunity that ultimately changed the course of my life.

It was also Judy who helped secure a car for the welfare—a worn white pick-up truck with "Child Welfare" boldly emblazoned on the side. The truck, with its faded paint and dented body, seemed almost symbolic of the organisation itself: imperfect, yet reliable and dedicated to its purpose. Ironically, it was in this very truck that I learned to drive as a teenager. Its engine often grumbled under the strain of age, becoming the backdrop for my first attempts behind the wheel. I can still recall gripping the steering wheel, the rough texture of the leather beneath my fingers, and the way the truck would jerk forward awkwardly as I fumbled with the pedals.

The welfare worker representing our small town was a black nun named Cecelia, and I adored her. She was unlike anyone I had ever met—strong, confident, and full of life. Despite her role, she was far from the stereotypical image of a nun. She didn't fit the mould of a quiet, solemn figure who adhered strictly to tradition. Instead, Cecelia was real and unapologetically herself in a world that often demanded conformity. Her presence was warm and comforting, her laugh infectious, and her spirit bold, unlike the reserved and distant figures I had been taught to expect.

At first, I found it odd that she would curse. The occasional expletive felt out of place for someone in her position. But soon I realised it made her seem more human, like someone who had seen and lived through things, not just a woman in a habit detached from the world's struggles. There was a fire in her, a passion that shone through in her words and actions, and which was impossible not to admire. She didn't hide behind a facade of piety—she was raw and open about her struggles, and that authenticity made her stand apart.

I remember hearing rumours about her secret boyfriend at one point. At first, I couldn't believe it, but then it made perfect sense. Cecelia wasn't someone to be confined by expectations. She lived in a way that balanced the demands of her role with the desires of her own heart. The fact that she could navigate this balance, blending the sacred and the worldly with such ease, made her even more remarkable in my eyes.

I admired her boldness and authenticity. She was someone who didn't force herself into any mould but instead forged her place in the world. Even though she represented an institution that often felt distant and rigid, Cecelia showed me that there was room for individuality within the confines of duty. She stood tall in her skin, embodying life's complexities without trying to fit into a box.

I often accompanied my mom and Cecelia on home visits, the three of us squeezed together in the cramped three-seater as we made our way up the rugged dirt road leading into one of the remote townships. The car bounced and creaked over the uneven path, dust swirling behind us in the heat of the day. Fires often burned in the distance, their acrid smoke thick in the air, while faint gunshots echoed like unsettling whispers, lingering in the atmosphere. It was a place alive with tension, where danger hung like a heavy cloud, threatening to burst at any moment. Certainly no place for three women, yet we ventured into it without hesitation.

The harsh, chaotic world outside stood in stark contrast to the calm inside the car, but I felt a strange sense of exhilaration as we drove deeper into it. It was exciting, yes, but also sobering. The township revealed a world filled with fear, danger, and deeply troubled lives. Children, their faces weary and haunted, sniffed glue to escape their grim reality. The homes we visited were filled with quiet despair—many of the cases involved orphaned children, child abuse, and families shattered by poverty. There was a pervasive sense of hopelessness, as though nothing would ever change.

Yet, despite the overwhelming sadness, I found myself fascinated. The rawness of it all, the human stories unfolding before us, drew me in. I watched every interaction with keen interest—every exchange between Cecelia, my mom, and the families we visited. It was a world I couldn't fully understand, but one I was deeply curious about.

There was always a sense of relief when we left the township, the dusty roads gradually fading into the distance as we returned to the relative safety of our world. The car's engine hummed a comforting tune, and the tension that had built up over the past hour slowly dissolved with each passing mile. I spent much of my free time at my mother's workplace, sorting through clothing, toys, and food donations that arrived by the truckload. The smells of worn fabric, fresh food, and a faint trace of antiseptic filled the air, creating a strange blend of comfort and sadness. Together, we carefully folded clothes and packed food into boxes to deliver to families in need. The rhythm of it felt almost meditative, as though the monotony of the task offered a way to escape the emotional weight of the visits.

It was fascinating to observe how people reacted to the donations—some faces would light up with gratitude, their eyes wide and thankful as they received the items, while others seemed distant, almost indifferent. A few felt entitled, questioning the quality of what we gave them, their voices tinged with surprise or irritation. My empathetic nature lingered on these interactions, trying to make sense of the complexities of human behaviour long after the fact. Why did some accept the gifts with grace while others resisted? What did it mean to truly help someone? I found myself reflecting on these questions as I watched the recipients, their expressions revealing far more than words ever could.

One case that stayed with me involved a family with a seven-year-old boy who could no longer attend school because his parents simply couldn't afford the fees. The pain in the mother's eyes as she spoke about her son's future haunted me. The helplessness in her voice was a stark reminder of how wide the divide between hope and despair could stretch. At the time, the South African education system was divided by race; a bitter reality. White schools, deemed "better" by the authorities, demanded high fees. In contrast, schools for coloured and black children either didn't charge fees at all or asked for far less—if they were even accessible at all. The injustice of it stung every time I thought about it. The faces of those locked out of opportunities, simply because of the colour of their skin, reflected the harshness of this divide.

The boy's future seemed bleak, solely due to the economic and racial barriers that separated him from the opportunities he deserved. He was just a child—bright, eager to learn, but trapped by forces far beyond his control. My mother and Cecelia tirelessly approached several white schools, their voices filled with desperation as they pleaded with administrators, only to face closed doors. They shared his story, hoping compassion would sway the hearts of those in charge, hoping the humanity of the situation would break through the rigid walls of bureaucracy. But every time, their pleas fell on deaf ears. I could almost feel the weight of their frustration pressing down on me. "The rules are the rules," they were told, and none of the schools were willing to bend them, no matter how heartbreaking the situation. The rejection felt like a slap—cold and unyielding. There was no space for compassion, no room for humanity to take precedence over the rules.

That cold rejection was a reminder of the harsh, impassable walls that divided people simply because of their race. Those walls weren't just physical—they were invisible, woven into the very fabric of society. The cruelty of it left me speechless. I was too young to fully grasp the magnitude of what I was witnessing, but the sting of injustice was undeniable. Even then, it felt like the world was showing me something deeply broken—something I didn't want to accept but couldn't ignore.

Finally, a coloured school—one of the many with fewer resources but a greater sense of community—welcomed him with open arms. The school wasn't perfect—it was worn, and overcrowded—but its doors were open, its heart open. For the first time in what felt like ages, there was a glimmer of hope for the boy. It wasn't the perfect solution, but it was a lifeline in a world that had been determined to deny him everything.

At first, it confused me. I couldn't understand how people, simply because of their skin colour, could be so heartless. How could anyone turn away someone who was simply trying to survive, trying to build a future? I was shocked by the indifference of those who had the means to help but chose not to. It was a cruelty I couldn't wrap my mind around as a child, but it shaped my understanding of the world in a way nothing else had.

This experience led me to deeply question the morality of white churches that refused to help anyone who wasn't white. The hypocrisy was suffocating, like a heavy cloud that blocked out any trace of truth or compassion. How could they claim to follow the teachings of love, compassion, and equality, yet deny aid to someone who was clearly in need? It felt like an unholy betrayal, a sin so cruel that it pierced through any semblance of righteousness they claimed to possess. The contradiction gnawed at me, and I couldn't understand how the very people who preached love could turn their backs on the suffering of others.

To me, it was an inhumane sin to deny assistance to someone desperately seeking help—for themselves, for their children, for their families. It was a contradiction at its worst—an example of how power and privilege could twist something as pure as faith into a tool of exclusion and oppression. The entitlement with which some judged others, without regard for the true meaning of their faith, disgusted me. It was a harsh awakening, but one that instilled a deep sense of injustice in my heart—a feeling I carried with me as I grew older, shaping my views on the world and religion.

Growing up during apartheid, I struggled with the way some white people treated black people—as though it was their right; as if their superiority was unquestionable. It felt like an unspoken rule that black people were inferior, and I saw it reflected in the way they were treated, as though their humanity didn't matter. The injustice was bitter, sinking deep into my bones, making me wrestle with silent objections I couldn't voice. Speaking out would have been seen not only as disrespectful but also as a betrayal of my race, a dangerous line to cross in a society that divided people so sharply. I found myself trapped between knowing what was right and fearing the consequences of speaking up. The conflict inside me was suffocating, like being caught in a vice between what I knew to be wrong and the expectations that society placed on me. Silence seemed like the safest option, but the cost of it weighed heavily on my conscience.

Yet, this period also marked the beginning of a shift within me. Something stirred deep inside, telling me I couldn't remain passive, and that I needed to question and challenge the world around me. I started becoming bolder, asking more questions, and challenging my parents on certain Bible verses, especially one like John 13:34: "A new commandment I give unto you, that ye love one another; as I have loved you, that ye also love one another."

These words burned within me, refusing to be ignored. I would ask, "How can we preach this, yet people are treated in such an inhumane way based on their skin colour?"

The questions grew like cracks in a dam, demanding answers. Though I couldn't always articulate my thoughts clearly, I instinctively understood the contradiction between what I was being taught and what I saw in the world. I've always questioned what I believe, even when it put me in a difficult position. At those moments, the gap between my teachings and the reality around me felt impossible to bridge.

But it wasn't just racism against black people that I witnessed. There was also a judgment against white people who didn't conform to the ways that the Holy Bible supposedly approved. It wasn't just about race—it was about fitting into a mould of righteousness defined by a select few. Anyone who didn't fit that mould was ostracised, judged, and cast aside.

In our small town, everyone knew everyone's business, and gossip spread like wildfire. One incident in particular shook me to my core—my Sunday school teacher, a woman who had always been kind and loving, was gang-raped by nine black men one evening and contracted AIDS. The news spread quickly, and the community's reaction was cruel. We were told not to accept hugs from her, and she was relegated to sitting alone on an entire church bench, isolated and rejected by the very people who should have been offering support.

This treatment blew my mind. We lived in a country where many people were infected with AIDS, and we had been educated on how the virus could or could not be contracted. Hugs were never listed as a risk. The community's reaction felt so unjust. She was a victim of a horrific crime, yet she was treated as if she had done something wrong. It felt like an additional layer of punishment, as if she had to pay for her trauma by having her humanity stripped away.

She, however, accepted it with grace. Her resilience, and her ability to bear such a heavy burden without lashing out, left me in awe. My inner self was torn between my anger at the injustice and my admiration for her grace.

I remember once defying the rules and giving her an embrace because I couldn't bear to see her so isolated. It wasn't about breaking any rules—it was about showing her that someone cared; that she wasn't invisible. I felt the disapproval in the air, thick as a storm, but it was the tear-filled eyes of my teacher that spoke volumes. At that moment, I felt a deep, silent connection between us—an understanding that needed no words. I wanted her to know that despite the cruelty she was enduring, there was one person in the room who saw her as human, who saw her pain, and still offered love.

Save Keeper

My father, in many ways, was my protector, simply through his presence. Quietly, I think my mom resented this, but I genuinely felt that she had to hold onto herself a little more when he was around. I often followed him around when he was home, doing whatever odd jobs he had to do. I would spend hours unpacking his toolbox, fascinated by the scraps of metal, old nails, and broken pieces of wood, creating makeshift projects while he worked in the garage. If he wasn't in the garage, he was working in the garden or mowing the lawn, and I'd sit nearby, either reading or drawing. It was in those moments that I felt most connected to him, watching him work and absorbing his calm, quiet energy.

My dad used to work at a prison, where he was both a warden and responsible for the medical care of prisoners. He carried a rifle as part of his duties and had to maintain his gun licence, which led to frequent trips to the shooting range. My brother and I always looked forward to these trips. We'd race to collect as many bullet casings as we could, the sharp metallic scent of gunpowder filling the air, mingling with the earthiness of the open outdoors. I loved everything about it—the wide-open space, the sound of shots echoing in the distance, and the feeling of being included in a world that was just for us.

But the most exciting part, of course, was when he would ask us if we wanted to try shooting. I remember the first time I held his handgun. It felt incredibly heavy in my small hands, and I recall how strangely powerful it felt to hold it, as though I was holding something capable of changing the world. I didn't like the feeling at all, but I thought it was cool, nonetheless. It was too powerful for me to shoot on my own, so my dad had to help hold it and protect me from the recoil. Guns were a normal part of life growing up in South Africa. We always had one under the driver's seat, no matter where we travelled, the presence of it a quiet constant in our daily lives.

Growing up on a prison base had its perks. The military occasionally landed their Chinooks on the prison grounds, and when they did, it was like an open invitation for all the kids to get a free ride. These announcements always came suddenly, and we had to run to catch the opportunity before the helicopters left. As a young child, this was thrilling. Looking back, I appreciate that there was little thought given to health and safety, because it allowed for so many experiences that would have otherwise never happened—memories that, in their reckless spontaneity, shaped my childhood in ways I didn't fully realise at the time.

There were also frequent escapes at the prison, which would trigger eerie alarms in the middle of the night or early morning. This was terrifying as a child, especially because it often ended in gunshots that could be heard even at the houses. We had to learn to fall to the floor and remain there until we were told it was safe again. Adrenaline would keep me awake, my heart racing in my chest, and I always worried about whether I would see my dad again, whether he would come home safe.

One event I recall that was particularly traumatic occurred during a hostage situation. It happened during the day, because I remember my brother and I being pulled out of school for our safety. The worst part was that no-one would give us any information, which only made everything feel worse. Later, we learned that it wasn't just prisoners who had held my dad and some co-workers captive, but other co-workers who had instigated it. My dad was badly beaten, and though it wasn't discussed much with us as children, I think the stress from the incident led to many changes in him. His working hours decreased after the incident, and eventually he took early retirement.

As a child, I was keenly aware that my dad wore two masks. To me, he rarely lost his temper or showed a mean streak. I know he might have been disappointed that I wasn't your typical girly girl, someone who loved wearing dresses. Instead, I was more of a tomboy— always climbing trees, building forts, and running around in the dirt. Still, he wasn't harsh in expressing his wish for me to act more like a girl.

I loved joining him and his friends on spontaneous fishing trips in the late afternoon. His friends had sons, and we shared a wonderful friendship, so the trips were always enjoyable and relaxing. As the sun set, we would catch crabs running out of the smaller waves, their little legs scrambling, and eat them by a fire made from driftwood on the beach. We'd spend a few hours there, the salty breeze tugging at our clothes, then drive back late at night, the sky full of stars that seemed to stretch on forever.

Sometimes, I also witnessed strange things, like when a man my dad knew from work helped clear up a massive crash on the motorway. I was with my dad, or nearby, when I overheard this man telling my dad about a fatal accident in which several people lost their lives. For some reason, the man had taken one of the severed limbs from the crash and kept it in the back of his trunk.

I'm not sure what disturbed me more—the sight of the arm, which was unsettling enough as a child, or the way the man spoke about it with disrespect and laughter. What troubled me the most was that my dad didn't voice his outrage or disapproval. He simply listened and allowed the conversation to unfold, offering only murmurs in response. He didn't call the man out for his callousness. At that moment, I felt deeply disappointed in my dad, inwardly embarrassed to be a part of this, and overwhelmed by a strange sense of detachment from everything around me. It was as if the man's words were contagious, and I was unable to separate myself from them. It was the first time I truly felt the weight of indifference—something that I would later recognise in myself.

The Quiet Ripple of a Once-Stirred Thought

My earlier life was a constant balancing act, always tiptoeing around my mother's moods, never knowing when the ground beneath me might suddenly give way. The sense of unease was omnipresent, like a storm cloud perpetually hanging above, on the verge of breaking, ready to unleash its fury at the slightest provocation. Every day felt like walking on a razor's edge, my body forever tense, as if I might be swallowed whole by the very air itself. I lived in a state of heightened awareness, always scanning her face for the smallest flicker of emotion—a twitch of the lip, a narrowing of the eyes—that might signal danger, a brewing storm ready to ravage the fragile calm of my world.

Monkey was there through it all, a silent witness to the quiet chaos that was my life. His small, stuffed body absorbed my tears and whispered fears, the soft, familiar fabric a comforting constant against my trembling hands. When her voice rose, sharp and cutting, I clutched him so tightly that his seams began to fray, his once-spotless fur now worn and faded from the endless grip of my desperate need for comfort. He wasn't just a toy; he was my anchor, my safety, my sanity in a world that felt like it could shatter at any moment.

Her punishments were relentless, her rage unpredictable, like a flash flood—sudden, overwhelming, and capable of sweeping everything away in its path. Homework was the worst. I sat at the kitchen table, bathed in the harsh, clinical light of the overhead lamp, the shadows of the night creeping into the corners of the room like dark vines. My fingers trembled as I tried to steady my pencil, each line of writing a fragile attempt at normalcy in a world that had none. If I struggled with an assignment, if my answers didn't meet her impossible standards, her anger erupted like a volcano, leaving me buried beneath its heat.

"How can you not get it?" she snapped, her voice slicing through the air, sharp as broken glass. "You'll never amount to anything." Her words were daggers, sharp and precise, and they stuck in my chest long after she had spoken them.

The sound of her hand slamming on the table rang in my ears like a gunshot, each strike reverberating through my entire body, while I fought to hold back tears, the overwhelming weight of shame and fear pressing down on my chest like a physical weight.

The smallest infractions were enough to unleash her fury—an uneven bedspread, clothes not folded to her exacting specifications. A forgotten chore could lead to her yanking my hair so violently that my scalp burned with pain, her fingers clamped like an iron vice. Sometimes, she would throw whatever was nearest—a hairbrush, a book—sending them crashing into the walls or the floor, each object adding to the chaos that spun around me, a reflection of the turmoil inside. It wasn't just the physical pain that stayed with me; it was the words that accompanied it, words that lingered in my mind like poison, seeping into my soul long after the bruises had faded.

"Child of a whore," she spat, her voice venomous and cold.

The phrase hit me like a slap; a sharp sting that echoed deep in my chest, leaving a hollow, aching emptiness. I didn't understand what it meant, didn't know who she was speaking of. Was she talking about my biological mother? I barely knew anything about the woman who gave birth to me, only that she wasn't in my life. The thought stung in ways I couldn't articulate, a deep, tangled knot of shame, confusion, and longing that twisted inside me, gnawing at my heart. Even as I carried an almost instinctual sense of protection for this woman I'd never met, those words made me question who I was and made me feel like something broken, something unworthy of love or peace.

As the years passed, the physical punishments lessened, but the verbal ones dug in, burrowing deep into my psyche, insidious and far more lasting. My mother didn't need to raise her hand anymore; her words did all the damage. They became my constant companions, echoing in my mind long after she'd left the room, a cruel refrain I couldn't escape. Sometimes, I sat on the edge of my bed with Monkey, squeezing him tightly as I replayed her insults, searching for answers, trying to understand why she hated me so much, why she seemed determined to destroy me from the inside out.

The thought of self-harm crossed my mind more times than I cared to admit, but I was too terrified of her reaction to ever act on it. Instead, I found other ways to feel pain—ways I could control. I rode my bike recklessly, racing down steep hills at breakneck speeds, almost daring myself to crash, to feel something, anything, other than the suffocating numbness that hung over me. Scraped knees, bruised elbows—they became my strange kind of comfort, a fleeting reminder that I was still alive, still here, even if it didn't always feel like it. The pain from these injuries, though sharp, was momentary, gone by the next day, unlike the emotional wounds that seemed to last forever.

Monkey was always there when I returned battered and bruised but somehow lighter, as if I had shed a bit of the heaviness that had weighed me down. I would sit on my bed, pressing him to my chest, and tell him everything. "At least this hurt makes sense," I whispered to him. "At least this kind of pain goes away." And somehow, for just a moment, I believed it. I believed in the simplicity of physical pain, in its ability to fade with time, unlike the deep, unresolved ache inside me that lingered long after the bruises had healed.

As I grew older, my hopes began to shift. I stopped wishing for the mother I once imagined, the kind and loving figure who would sweep in and make everything better. That fragile hope, once so vivid, withered and died as I came to realise that it was never going to happen. Instead, my wishes became simpler and more desperate. I began to hope that my adopted mother would find a full-time job, something that would keep her away from the house for hours at a time, something to break the suffocating monotony of her presence. But she stayed, always there, always watching, always hovering, determined to present herself to the outside world as the caring, present mother.

The contrast between the person she showed to others and the one I knew at home was maddening, like two different worlds colliding. Around neighbours, teachers, and family friends, she was all smiles and gentle words, her voice syrupy sweet. "Roux is such a bright girl," she would say, her tone dripping with pride, her eyes gleaming with an almost sickening satisfaction. Every time I heard those words, it felt like a slap across my face, a cruel reminder of the lies she wove so effortlessly. But I knew better than to speak out, knew that doing so would only make things worse. I had learned long ago that silence was my only refuge, the only way to avoid the storm.

This was my life, well into my teenage years. By then, I had stopped dreaming of rescue. I no longer looked for escape routes or imagined a different life. Instead, I felt trapped, suffocated by the constant tension that hung in the air like smoke. The invisible weight of her presence was always with me, even when she wasn't in the room. Her voice echoed in my mind, a constant reminder of the harshness that lived within me, in the space between each breath.

Monkey remained my only solace, my one connection to something pure and unchanging in a world that had none. I didn't care that I was too old to carry a stuffed animal around. Monkey was more than that. He was a witness to my life, a keeper of my secrets, a reminder that not everything in my world had to be sharp and cruel. When everything else felt unstable, I knew I could turn to him and find, if only for a moment, something soft, something safe.

At night, when the house was silent and the darkness pressed in around me, I would lie in bed with Monkey tucked under my chin. His worn fur, soft against my skin, was the only comfort I had in a life that offered so little. I would whisper my thoughts to him, knowing he would never betray me, never use my words against me.

"I don't know how much longer I can do this," I told him one night, my voice barely audible in the stillness. "But I have to, right? Because no-one's coming to save me."

I understood that now with crystal clarity. No-one was coming. There was no fairy tale ending waiting for me, no knight in shining armour to rescue me from this tower. It was just me and Monkey, weathering the storm together, as we always had.

And so, together, we endured.

Across the Lap's Tender Horizon

The room is calm, warm, and peaceful. The blinds are partially opened, letting in some outside light. There's a sense of neutrality here. The air is thick with a grounding, earthy scent—a blend of aged wood and the faint, comforting musk of earth—that fills the space and lingers like an old memory. It's the kind of scent that both soothes and excites, settling deep in my chest and making my heart race, just as it always does in this place.

I stand beside her, still and attentive, hands clasped in front of me, the anticipation building with every passing second. She sits in a chair across the room, poised yet relaxed, her gaze sharp, steady, and intent. Her eyes study me, equal parts warmth and command, holding me in their gaze as if she knows exactly who I am, exactly what I need.

"Ready?" Her voice is soft, almost a whisper, but it rings clear in the stillness. She pats her lap with both hands, the sound deliberate, creating a quiet rhythm that echoes in the room, pulling at the very core of me. It's a signal—one we both understand without words—that it's time: time for me to step forward, to give myself over to her, to the moment.

I step toward her, my hands already damp with the suspense of what's to come. The air feels heavier now, thick with expectation. I drape myself over her lap, settling into the familiar position, my body relaxing instinctively. Her hands are firm yet gentle as they adjust me, one resting lightly on the small of my back, a silent reassurance.

She begins slowly, her hand meeting my skin with rhythmic precision. The first few strikes are a warm-up, the initial slaps gentle yet purposeful, sending a surge of warmth spreading across my skin. The sound is soft at first—slap, slap, slap—a sound that mirrors the even rhythm of my breath. It's not painful, not yet. It's a steady, gradual build, a grounding pulse that lets me settle into the moment, into the sensation.

"Relax," she murmurs, her voice low and soothing, like a balm for my restless mind. I close my eyes, the words fading away as I focus on the rhythmic sensation—the way her hand never misses its mark, the steady heat rising, seeping into me with each strike. The tension in my shoulders begins to ease, replaced by a strange, almost meditative calm that flows through me, grounding me in the present.

"Right, I'm going to switch to the paddle," she says, the soft rustle of movement preceding her words. For a moment, her hand pauses, and then I feel the familiar weight of a leather paddle in her hand. The shift is palpable, the feel of the paddle against my skin different—more solid, more resonant. The impact is deeper now, each strike pulling a soft gasp from my lips, but I don't flinch. This is what I asked for. This is what I wanted.

"Okay," I say, my voice trembling yet filled with quiet conviction. I've spoken about this desire before, pushing her to test my limits, to see just how far I can go. She always listens and always checks, but I trust her with this. I trust her to take me to places that I can't reach on my own.

The strikes come harder now, sharper, the sound of the paddle meeting my skin echoing in the room. My fingers grip her knee, seeking some form of anchor as the intensity rises, the sting spreading in a vibrant wave across my body. With each strike, I feel the sting intensify, a sharp contrast to the underlying warmth that lingers beneath.

As the intensity builds, so too does the pressure in my chest, the air growing thicker with each strike. My palms grow slick with sweat, and my breathing is shallow, but I push past it. She notices the shift, as always, and takes my wrist in a firm grip, holding it against my back. The gesture sends a flutter through my stomach—a reminder that she is in control, that I am safe, even as my body trembles beneath her touch.

"You're doing so well," she murmurs, her voice a gentle reassurance amidst the storm of sensation.

I nod, biting my lip to stifle the sounds I long to make. The next set comes faster, sharper, and relentless, each strike landing with a precision that makes my vision blur with the intensity. My hands sweat, my breath catches in my throat, and for a brief moment, I wonder if I can take any more. But I trust her. I know she is watching me, reading my body, ready to catch me if I fall.

When she finally stops, her hand rests gently on my lower back, grounding me once more.

"Breathe," she says softly, her voice tender and calm. "Have a sip of water."

I exhale shakily, the tension that had built up in my body slowly unravelling under the touch of her hand. She doesn't rush me, doesn't demand anything. She simply lets me lie there, allowing the space to process, to find my way back to myself.

"You did so well," she says again, her voice full of pride, and it fills me with warmth. She lifts me gently, helping me to stand, her hand steady on my arm, guiding me as I regain my balance.

"Thank you," I whisper, my voice hoarse but full of gratitude.

Her smile is soft and knowing, and it makes my chest ache with something deeper than words can explain.

"Always," she says, her voice a promise. "You're safe here."

And in that moment, I know I am. For all the intensity, for all the testing of limits, I feel seen, understood, and most of all safe. Even as my skin tingles and my body still trembles from the experience, I know that here, in this space, I am whole.

The Letter

I sit in my room, surrounded by the quiet stillness, the soft afternoon light filtering through the window and gently illuminating the space around me. I'm perched awkwardly on the edge, trying not to wrinkle the neatly made comforter, which my mother would undoubtedly notice if disturbed. Across the room, my parents are leaning over the desk, sorting through an endless stack of papers—tax forms, insurance documents, receipts—mundane adult things I usually have no interest in.

But then something catches my eye.

My mother reaches into a folder and pulls out some papers. Beneath a cream-coloured envelope with the words "Adopted Parents" written neatly across the top, they are visible. My heart skips a beat. I watch as she skim through the papers, casually tossing them onto a growing pile before shifting her focus to another stack. My father asks something about deductions, but I barely hear him. All my attention is fixed on that envelope.

It isn't just the title, though that alone sends my mind racing; it's the way my mother doesn't even glance at it. The envelope lies there like just another piece of paper, but something deep inside me tells me otherwise. A sudden heat rises in my chest, a mixture of curiosity and something I can't quite name.

I stay quiet, forcing myself to appear uninterested, but my fingers twitch against the bedspread. Is it about me? Does it have something to do with my adoption? It has to. My heart thuds in my chest as I replay the sight of the envelope in my mind. "Adopted Parents" —the words feel heavy, almost sacred.

I don't dare ask about it. If I do, my mother will either brush me off or hide it away, ensuring I'll never see it again. So instead, I wait, biding my time, my eyes darting occasionally to the pile where the envelope lies. I don't look directly at it for too long, not wanting to draw attention, but I memorise its location—top of the stack, slightly crooked, the cream colour stark against the plain white papers below.

A few days later, the opportunity presents itself. The house is empty—my parents are out running errands, and my brother is at a friend's place. I sit on the couch, pretending to watch TV, but my mind is elsewhere. I've been waiting for this moment, counting down the minutes until I'm alone.

Quietly, I creep upstairs to my parents' bedroom. My hands are clammy, and my breath is quick and shallow as I close the door behind me. The desk where the papers had been sorted sits against the far wall, its surface still cluttered. My eyes scan the piles, searching frantically. For a moment, panic grips me. What if they've moved it? What if it's gone?

But then I see it—tucked beneath a few sheets of paper, a corner of the cream-coloured envelope peeking out— just enough to make my heart leap. I rush over, my hands trembling as I pull it free.

The words "Adopted Parents" stare back at me, and I hesitate for a moment, my stomach twisting. I know this is wrong. I know I'm not supposed to see this. But something deeper, something primal, urges me forward. I slide my finger under the flap and pull out the letter inside.

The handwriting is perfect, looping and graceful, each word written with care. My eyes scan the page, my breath hitching as I read.

Dear Adopted Parents,

I'm writing this letter to thank you for giving my baby a home, a life, a chance. I was only sixteen when I gave birth to her. Her name was Roux. She's yours now, but I wanted you to know how much I loved her. How much I still love her.

My throat tightens, my vision blurring as my eyes race over the page.

Her father wasn't ready for a family, and he left before she was born. I tried to imagine raising her on my own, but I knew I couldn't give her the life she deserved. It was the hardest decision I've ever made, but I wanted to give her the best chance at happiness. I hope she knows that. I hope she knows this wasn't easy for me. That I loved her enough to let her go.

My hands shake as I clutch the letter, my heart pounding so loudly I can barely hear my thoughts. The words are alive, vibrating with warmth and honesty, each one a thread connecting me to a woman I've never met but suddenly feel I know—my birth mother.

There's no anger in the letter, no bitterness. Only love— pure, unwavering love—that leaps off the page and wraps itself around me like a warm embrace. I feel it, deep in my chest, a feeling so powerful it leaves me breathless.

My gaze lingers on the final lines:

Please tell her I loved her. Please tell her I always will. Thank you for giving her what I couldn't.

I press the letter to my chest, tears streaming down my face. I don't know how long I sit there, holding the paper as though it's a lifeline, a bridge to the mother I've never known. It's magical, this connection that crackles like lightning, filling me with a warmth I haven't felt in years.

Over the weeks that follow, the letter becomes my secret treasure. Every time the house is empty, I slip into my parents' room, retrieve the envelope, and read the letter again. I memorise every word, tracing the loops of my mother's handwriting with my finger, marvelling at how perfect it is. I imagine my birth mother sitting down to write it, the care and love she must have poured into every stroke of the pen.

The letter becomes my escape, my solace. In a house that often feels cold and hostile, it's a reminder that somewhere, someone loved me unconditionally. It doesn't matter that she's a stranger; she feels closer to me than anyone else in the world.

Each time I hold the letter, I feel something indescribable, as though I'm cradling a piece of her soul. It's the only thing I have of her; the only connection to a past that's always felt like a shadowy mystery.

I imagine what she's like. My mind paints her as beautiful, kind, and strong. Someone who would have held me tightly, whispered words of comfort when I cried, celebrated my triumphs, and wiped away my tears. In my mind, she is everything my adoptive mother isn't.

I begin to dream of her—vivid dreams where we meet in fields of wildflowers or at cozy kitchen tables, talking for hours. I wake up smiling, the warmth of those imagined moments lingering even after the dreams fade.

One day, as I read the letter for the tenth, maybe twentieth, time, I caught my reflection in the mirror above the dresser. My tear-streaked face stares back at me, and for a moment, I see her. The thought startles me, a pang of longing coursing through me. I want to meet her, to hear her voice, to tell her that I understand, that I feel her love.

But deep down, I know I can't. The letter is the closest I'll ever get to my birth mother. And maybe that's enough.

As I carefully fold the letter and slip it back into its envelope, I feel a sense of peace I haven't known before. My mom gave me up because she loved me. Because she wanted me to have a better life.

And while that life is far from perfect, I cling to the hope that someday, I might make it better. For her. For myself.

The Black Sheep

At sixteen, the room feels like a museum of someone I barely remember: a faded floral bedspread; curling posters of places I once dreamed of visiting; and shelves cluttered with forgotten trinkets—old trophies, empty picture frames, and knickknacks that have long since lost their significance. Each item seems to echo a version of me that has slipped further and further away. I sit cross-legged on my bed, a textbook sprawled open in my lap, its pages filled with words that refuse to stick. They blur together, meaningless shapes, like trying to read through a dense fog that won't lift.

The weight in my chest is suffocating, thick like smoke, pressing harder with every passing minute. I haven't spoken to my mom in two days, but that's nothing new. We pass each other in the house like ghosts, barely acknowledging each other, our conversations limited to the bare necessities, as though words are a rare commodity we can't afford. The silence between us hangs like a thick, suffocating fog, and it's not just the absence of words—it's the absence of warmth. This isn't a new silence; it's been growing for years, slowly accumulating until it suffocates everything. The relationship between us isn't strained. It's shattered. Fragments scattered so far apart that there's no hope of ever piecing them back together.

Where there was once screaming, there's now cold indifference. And that indifference, I've learned, cuts deeper than any slap or shout ever did. It's a silent, gnawing pain that claws at my insides, leaving behind an emptiness so deep I can feel it in my bones. The void between us is an abyss, and the silence between our words feels more suffocating than any sound ever could.

The yelling stopped when I was thirteen. The slaps, the hair-pulling—they simply ceased, as if someone had flipped a switch. Maybe it was because I'd grown too old to be thrown around. Maybe marks on a teenager are harder to explain. Or maybe she'd just grown tired of the physical effort. I don't know, and I don't ask. It happened so suddenly, leaving me disoriented, hollowed out, unsure of where the pain had gone, but also unsure of who I was without it. The absence of pain left a strange, unsettling void in its place, and I've never really known what to do with it.

For years, the pain had been almost... grounding. A twisted comfort, in its own way. It was pain I could understand, pain that followed a cause and came with an effect. When her hand struck my arm, or when my scalp burned from her grip, I knew exactly why it happened. But now, the absence of that pain leaves me floundering, adrift. Without it, her anger is a quieter monster—still sharp, but subtler, hidden in her words instead of her blows. It's not something I can escape, not something I can make sense of.

"You're impossible, Roux," she said last night. One of the only things she's said to me all week. Her voice wasn't loud, just clipped and dry, like I was something she'd forgotten to deal with until the moment she saw me. "You act like the world owes you something. It doesn't."

I didn't argue. I swallowed the words that rose in my throat, letting her comment sink deep like a stone dropped into still water. There's no point in fighting. Not anymore. I realised long ago that fighting only made it worse. It was a futile effort. So, I stayed silent, the weight of her words pressing into me like a stone lodged in my chest.

The textbook slides from my lap, landing with a soft thud against the bedspread as I lean back. My eyes wander upward, tracing the swirls in the plaster ceiling, watching as they twist and shift like storm clouds gathering. The patterns in the ceiling seem to shift, mirroring the way my mind churns and roils, unable to find peace. The darkness in my head isn't sadness. It's something deeper, something more suffocating. It creeps through the cracks in my thoughts, waiting patiently, lingering in the spaces between my breath, always there, always waiting to drag me under.

I don't cry anymore. I used to. Tears used to spill over easily, coming in waves at the slightest harsh word or cold glare. But now, my chest feels hollow, like there's nothing left to give. The pain builds, layer upon layer, with no escape. It presses down on me until I feel like I can't breathe. I try to distract myself—schoolwork, music, reading—but it's always there, lurking, waiting for the quiet moments to pull me under again, to drown me in its weight.

The door to my room is cracked just enough to let in the muffled voices from the living room. I don't mean to listen, but her voice cuts through the air immediately, sharp and unmistakable. She's talking to my brother. Every instinct tells me to stop, to turn away, but I can't. I know this beat, this rhythm. I've heard it all before.

"I don't know what to do with her," my mom says. Her voice is low, but I can feel the weight of her frustration in it. "She's just... so difficult. Everything's a fight. It's like she wants to make my life harder."

My throat tightens. My hands curl into fists, nails biting into my palms, but I don't move. Her words keep coming, each one sharper, more cutting than the last. They slice through me, carving open wounds I thought had healed. The anger and the hurt rise inside me, but I stay still, frozen, because I know that no matter how hard I try to fight back, it won't make any difference.

"God has a reason for everything," she says, bitterness lining her words. "But I don't get what His reason is for her."

The silence that follows feels deafening. Her words echo in my head, looping over and over until they drown out every other sound. *I don't get what His reason is for her.*

Something inside me cracks and solidifies all at once, a strange collision of breaking and hardening. I step back from the door, my breath shallow, each inhale heavier than the last. Deep down, I've always known she felt this way. But hearing it aloud, hearing her say it so plainly, is like the ground being ripped out from under me. It's a truth I didn't want to face.

I sink onto the bed, gripping the edge of the mattress as though it might steady me. I want to cry, but no tears come. I sit there, numb, as her words settle like stones in the hollow spaces of my chest. I tell myself I don't need her love. *You don't need anyone's love*, I think, repeating the words like a mantra. *You're on your own.*

It's both terrifying and liberating. For years, I clung to the fragile hope that things might change. That she might change. That the love I craved so desperately might somehow find its way to me. But now, that hope is gone. And with it, the weight of trying to fix it, to earn something that was never going to come.

I don't need it anymore.

That night, I lie awake, staring at the ceiling as the patterns in the plaster swirl above me. Monkey sits on the pillow beside me, his button eyes catching the faint glow of the streetlamp outside. I haven't spoken to him in months. Somewhere along the way, I stopped believing in anything or anyone that might make me feel safe. But now, without thinking, I reach for him. My fingers brush against his worn, frayed fur, and I pull him close, pressing his small, threadbare body against my chest.

"Fuck it," I whisper into the darkness. "I'm done trying to make her love me."

My voice doesn't waver. It's steady, flat. It doesn't feel like a decision. It feels like survival.

In the weeks that follow, I change. I stop trying to please her. I stop bending over backward to avoid her wrath. When she snaps at me, I don't flinch. When my brother tries to talk to me, I brush him off. I build walls—thick, impenetrable walls—and keep everyone at arm's length. It's easier this way. Safer.

But the darkness doesn't go away. It coils tighter, wrapping itself around my thoughts, whispering things I can't unhear. *You're unlovable. You're broken. You'll always be alone.* My darkest months by far.

I became so cold, so distant, and so consumed by anger at the world. It felt like a thick, impenetrable fog settled over me, one that made everything seem distant and unreachable. The word "mother" burned like acid in my stomach, sharp and bitter, a reminder of all that had been taken from me. At that moment, I lost it. I felt an explosive, raw anger toward my birth mother—for not trying, for not owning her mistakes, for leaving me in this place of emotional ruin. I couldn't even look at the idea of her without bitterness clawing at my chest.

She is nothing like me, I would say, the words bitter on my tongue. *If she were,* I would think, *she would prove the world wrong and fight for me.* She should have fought for me. She should have found a way to make it right, to choose me. But she didn't.

The scenes I once played out in my head—the ones where she returned for me, where she apologised and begged for forgiveness—are now different. Instead of the soft, tear-filled reunions I once longed for, when she comes for me in my thoughts, I now ask her to leave. I ask her to never come for me again, to never take up space in my heart or my mind. I don't want her there anymore. The damage is too deep, the anger too overwhelming, and the absence she left is too much to bear.

I want her to feel the same pain I've felt. I want her to carry the weight of the emptiness she left behind, to understand the ache of abandonment that's twisted inside me. In my heart, something has changed—I've become heartless. The compassion I once had is gone, replaced by a cold resolve. I don't care anymore. I don't care about the reasons, the excuses, or the apologies that will never come. All I care about now is the justice of seeing her hurt, to feel what I've been carrying for so long.

At that moment, I went searching for the envelope— the last piece of hers I still had. Her letter, her words—fragments of a past I had tried to forget. I tore it apart, my hands shaking as I shredded the only connection I had left to her. The paper crumpled beneath my fingers like a symbol of everything I had lost. It was an act of defiance, of destruction, but also an act of reclaiming control.

At that point, I learned something about myself. I learned that I can hurt, bleed even, and still stand. The rawness of the pain was almost suffocating, but it didn't break me. It wasn't the kind of pain that shattered; it was the kind that carved a space inside me, one that I could fill with something stronger. This level of pain, excruciating and relentless, almost carries a sense of empowerment. It's a bitter truth—that I can endure this, survive it, and come out the other side. I may be scarred, but I am still here.

This shaped my teenage years in ways I can't ignore. It moulded me into someone unrecognisable, someone who developed a "fuck it" attitude—a survival instinct. I started taking pleasure in pushing my mother further, taunting the monster inside her, daring it to come out and face me. *Do your worst*, I'd think. *Do the best damage you possibly can.* Her words, the ones she used to break me, no longer had the power to wound—they fed my walls, turning them into something harder, something like steel. They grew thicker and stronger with each insult, each put-down.

Before, I had tried to understand her. I tried to reason, to find a way to make sense of her cruelty. But now—it's different. Now, it's no longer about finding understanding. It's become a badge of strength, a declaration of resilience. A statement of power. I know her well enough now that my goal is no longer to please her or to seek her approval. No, now I want to get under her skin, make her lose control, and watch her fall apart in moments of pure rage. I'm not here to prove myself anymore, not here to earn little badges of affection I'll never get.

Now, it's about owning my strength.

Judicial

It's a crisp November morning, Friday, with another busy work week behind me. Today feels different as I prepare for the drive to my Mistress. My mind is surprisingly calm and clear, a stark contrast to the usual chaos. Even though our last session left it in overdrive, processing countless memories and thoughts, I feel a strange peace. Not all of them were bad—just long-buried fragments unearthed from the chaos of what once was.

As I pull into the driveway and park, a sudden flutter stirs in my stomach. For once, I know exactly what I want from this session. No warm-up, no safety net of OTK (Over The Knee); just a cold caning. The thought sends a shiver down my spine. I feel an overwhelming urge to retreat into my head, to focus and let go of the stress that's been weighing me down. This is what I've been craving—something sharp and intense to cut through the fog.

Before I can knock, she opens the door and welcomes me in. She's dressed, as always, in her signature black dress and high heels, the stark simplicity of it grounding me. There's something about the structure of it that I find both reassuring and commanding. I follow her upstairs, where we sit down for a quick conversation.

I always enjoy these moments—short but vivid, with just a few words painting pictures that don't need to be explained. By now, I feel she understands me, this journey I'm on, in a way no-one else ever has.

As usual, she asks the question that cuts through the air: "What are you looking for today?"

I hesitate.

"The usual? Only OTK... maybe the bench?" I hear her voice, calm but firm.

Fuck it, I think, and blurt out the question instead. "Could I have a cold caning session?"

"Of course, you can," she replies, her tone steady but assured. "It's called a judicial," she explains with a slight pause. "It will still be sets of six, but slower."

Relief washes over me—no further explanation is needed. She prepares the bench as I undress, taking a final sip of water. The room feels cool, though I know she prefers it that way, in contrast to my love for heat. It won't matter soon; I know the clamminess will set in.

I don't feel like talking as I mentally prepare myself. The silence hangs thick in the air, the kind that feels almost sacred. I take my position, determined to stay in it until the end. I hear her selecting her first cane, the subtle sound of her movements beside me. By now, I know she's right-handed; the strongest blows always come from that side.

The cane slices through the air as she warms up, its whistle sharpening my focus. The anticipation builds with each tap against my skin, a gesture I've come to expect but never fully understand. Is she taking aim, or is she teasing me, building the suspense? Either way, I love how it makes my heart race, pulling me into the present moment, and making everything else fall away.

This session is silent—no counting. I find myself wondering if this is intentional or if she, too, is deeply focused. Her voice, usually so calming, is absent, leaving me alone in the stillness. There's something powerful about this silence, about being in a space where words aren't necessary.

She changes the cane multiple times during the session; it's never the same. She always moves with a composed purpose, always in control. The change of cane gives me a moment to relax, but not for long. Sometimes, I'm so deeply focused it feels as though the outside world no longer exists.

She's preparing to bring the session to an end now, holding my favourite cane, the one with the black handle. Her movements are deliberate, and full of purpose, signalling the final moments. I'm ready, exhausted but fulfilled. I stay still, savouring the rawness of my body, the surrender that's about to come.

As I slowly rise, I feel the familiar rush of sensations—intense, like a cascade of warmth and heat coursing through me. It's like a volcano erupting inside, fierce and unrelenting, but in a way that's cleansing, purifying. This is what I love most about the ending: the natural high that follows, overwhelming and intense, like it's sweeping away everything else.

We finish with a hug. I still struggle with this part sometimes, especially when I feel the tears building. The emotion swells, unexpectedly, bringing with it a mix of sadness, emptiness, and release. But her tight embrace makes it okay to let go. I surrender to the moment, allowing the tears to come, feeling them pour out like the last bit of weight I've been carrying.

When I'm ready to release her, I feel a flash of embarrassment at having been so vulnerable in front of someone. Even though I know she understands completely, I wish she wouldn't look at me right then. But at the same time, I don't want to be left alone, not yet, not while I'm still untangling everything that just happened.

We say our goodbyes, and just like that, we vanish back into our separate lives.

Semicolon

The house is unusually quiet, the only sound the faint hum of the refrigerator and the ticking of the clock in the kitchen, each second stretching out longer than the last. I sit cross-legged on the worn sofa, flipping through the channels on the television without any real intention of watching anything. It's the kind of idle distraction that never fully occupies my mind.

Ryan, my brother, sprawls out on the armchair across the room, flicking through the pages of his book, his expression unreadable. He might as well not even be there. Our parents are at a parents' evening at school—the kind of event I loathe. The thought of my mother speaking to my teachers, putting on that sickeningly sweet facade of a doting parent, makes my stomach churn.

The tension between Ryan and me is palpable, simmering just beneath the surface. It's been this way for weeks, small annoyances stacking on top of each other like a precarious tower of cards. And tonight, it takes just one small push to send it tumbling.

"Can you stop clicking through channels like that?" Ryan mutters, not even looking up from his book.

I glare at him from the couch, my thumb deliberately pressing the remote to flip through another set of meaningless shows, as if I'm trying to provoke him. "What's your problem?" I snap. "It's not like you're watching anything."

Ryan scoffs, finally looking up. "You're so annoying, Roux. Can't you just, I don't know, sit still for five minutes?"

My jaw tightens, the familiar knot of anger rising in my chest. "Oh, I'm annoying? You're the one sitting there acting like a king while I can't even change the stupid channel."

"God, you always have to make everything about you," he shoots back, his voice rising. "It's exhausting."

The argument escalates quickly, our voices ricocheting off the walls of the empty house. The words we hurl at each other grow sharper, more personal. It doesn't matter that the fight started over something so trivial; it's become a battlefield, years of resentment and frustration boiling over in a single moment.

Ryan stands up, his face flushed with anger. "You know what? I wish you were never adopted into this family. I wish our parents never chose you."

The words hit me like a physical blow, knocking the air out of my lungs. For a moment, I just stare at him, unable to process what he's said. Then, the fury surges forward, masking the pain.

"Yeah? Well, I wish I wasn't adopted either!" I scream, my voice breaking. "You think I wanted to end up here? With you? With her?"

The silence that follows is deafening, our words hanging in the air like shards of broken glass. Ryan looks away, his jaw tightening, and mutters something under his breath before walking out of the room. I don't care enough to ask what he said. The damage is already done.

I stand there for a long moment, my chest heaving, my hands trembling at my sides. The silence feels oppressive now, pressing down on me like a weight I can't shake off. Ryan's words replay in my mind, looping over and over. *I wish you were never adopted into this family.*

I feel something crack inside me, a deep and hollow sound that echoes in the pit of my stomach. The anger that had flared so brightly just moments ago fizzles out, leaving behind an emptiness that feels unbearable, like a part of me has just shattered.

I move toward the stairs as though on autopilot, my feet dragging with each step. By the time I reach my bedroom, I feel like a ghost floating through the motions of someone else's life. The room is dimly lit, the soft glow of my bedside lamp casting long shadows on the walls, deepening the sense of isolation. Monkey sits on the edge of my bed, his button eyes dull in the muted light. I pick him up and cradle him against my chest, my fingers tracing the familiar worn patch on his arm.

"Fuck it," I whisper into the stillness, my voice sounding small and far away, as if I'm no longer the one speaking. It feels like it belongs to someone else.

I gently place Monkey back on the bed before leaving the room and heading to the top of the staircase where the medicine cabinet is kept. My hands tremble as I open the door and rummage through the clutter until my fingers close around a small blue pill bottle. I hold it up to the light, reading the label through blurry eyes. These are my hay fever pills, the ones I stopped taking because they were too strong, always leaving me drowsy.

I sit down on the edge of the bed, staring at the bottle in my hand. I unscrew the cap and pour all of the pills into my palm. They're small, green, nothing remarkable. I stare at them for a long time, the weight of the moment pressing down on me, but I feel no hesitation. *This is it,* I think. *My decision is final.* There is no tomorrow.

I swallow the pills all at once, my throat constricting as they go down. My hands are still shaking as I set the empty bottle on the nightstand. For a moment, I feel a flicker of something like doubt, a faint voice in the back of my mind telling me to stop, to reconsider. But it's drowned out by the darkness that has consumed me, the certainty that I stand by the decisions I make. There's no room for second thoughts now.

The room feels heavy, the air thick and suffocating, pressing in from all sides. I get up and head back to the medicine cabinet, reaching for another bottle of pills. The container is still sealed, but I rip away the seal without hesitation as if it's all become mechanical.

I pour them into my hand, swallow them down, and wait.

I lie back on the bed, staring up at the ceiling. My thoughts are slow now, muddled, like I'm sinking into a thick fog. My body grows heavier by the second, but there's a strange sense of calm in the heaviness, a quiet certainty that I don't have to fight anymore. I feel the pull of darkness, its weight wrapping around me like a blanket.

My last thought is not of regret or fear, but of release.

And then, there is nothing.

*

The world is a blur of light and noise when I wake up. My body feels heavy, my limbs unresponsive, and my mind swims in a haze that makes it impossible to think clearly. The first thing I notice is the sensation of hands—so many hands—gripping my arms, my legs, my shoulders. The bed beneath me feels cold, and foreign, and I instinctively try to pull away, but my body doesn't cooperate the way I want it to.

"Hold her still!" a voice barks, sharp and urgent. It takes me a moment to realise the voice isn't familiar. It isn't my mother's, or my father's, or my brother's. It's deeper and commanding, and as my head turns sluggishly to follow it, I'm met with the sight of white coats and blue scrubs.

I jerk again, panic flaring in my chest as I realise I can't move properly. The hands holding me down tighten, and I hear someone else say, "We need to get this in her now."

The confusion begins to shift into sharp embarrassment as I feel someone pulling at my waistband, exposing my backside. My face flushes hot, and I thrash harder, the effort sending shockwaves of pain through my body. "No! No!" I scream, though my voice cracks, hoarse and weak. I fight like a caged animal, desperately trying to escape.

"Roux, stop fighting!" one of the voices shouts, though I can't tell who's speaking. I crane my neck to look over my shoulder and see the needle, long and gleaming, in someone's hand. My heart pounds in my ears, drowning out the rest of the room's chaos.

Not like this, I think, a surge of defiance breaking through my disorientation. The idea of being held down, of being exposed like this in front of so many people, is unbearable. I kick my legs weakly, my movements erratic, but it's no use.

"Got it," someone says, and the sharp sting of the injection follows. My body seizes momentarily, and then the haze thickens, swallowing my panic whole.

The next time I open my eyes, the room is quieter. My head throbs, my stomach feels hollow and twisted, and my limbs are leaden. I'm in a hospital room now, sterile and white, the faint beeping of monitors the only sound. My throat burns, dry and raw, and when I try to move, a wave of nausea crashes over me.

I blink slowly, trying to piece together how I got here, but the memories are fragmented and slippery.

I remember the pills, the weight of them in my hand, the way my chest had felt so heavy, so certain. I remember lying down, thinking that was the end. But this... this wasn't supposed to happen.

Voices filter in from outside the room, muffled but intense. My parents' voices. I can tell by the sharp, defensive tone of my mother and the lower, almost pleading tone of my father.

"She wouldn't do that," my mother says, her voice tight. "Roux wouldn't, she wouldn't try to... to hurt herself."

"With the amount of pills she ingested, there's no question about her intent," another voice says, calm but firm. A doctor, maybe. "She's extremely lucky to be alive."

"Lucky?" My mother's voice cracks, a mix of disbelief and anger. "You're saying this was deliberate? No, you're wrong. She... she must have made a mistake. She wouldn't do this."

I squeeze my eyes shut, the sound of my mother's denial like shards of glass cutting into my already fragile mind. Of course, she doesn't believe it. Of course, she can't. I've spent years perfecting the art of hiding—hiding my pain, my anger, my despair. My mother's voice is sharp, almost shrill now, but it fades into the background as my exhaustion pulls me back under.

When I wake again, the room is darker. The lights have been dimmed, but I can still see the IV pole next to my bed, the faint outline of the heart monitor. My body feels strange and disconnected, as though it doesn't quite belong to me anymore. My skin feels hot and itchy, and my mouth tastes bitter and metallic. I turn my head slightly, my gaze landing on my mother sitting in the corner of the room.

She's staring out the window, her arms crossed tightly over her chest. She looks tired, her face drawn and pale. I blink, my vision swimming, and when I look again, my mother isn't sitting there anymore.

Instead, it's a boy—a boy I don't recognise, with dark hair and a soft smile. He's leaning forward, his elbows resting on his knees, watching me with a curious expression.

"Finally awake?" he says, his voice light, almost teasing.

I frown, my lips dry and cracked. "Who are you?" I croak, my voice barely above a whisper.

The boy doesn't answer. Instead, he tilts his head, his smile fading. "Why did you do it?" he asks, his tone softer now, almost sad.

"I..." My throat tightens, my mind racing to make sense of what I'm seeing. I don't answer. I can't.

When I blink again, he's gone, and my mother is back in the chair, staring at me with an unreadable expression.

"You've really done it this time, Roux," she says, her voice cold and distant.

I turn my head away, tears stinging my eyes. I don't know what's real anymore. The lines between reality and hallucination blur, leaving me adrift in a sea of confusion and fear. I try to speak, to ask if anyone else saw the boy, but the words catch in my throat. *If I tell them, they'll think I'm crazy*, I think, the idea sending a fresh wave of panic through me.

*

The days bleed together. Time no longer has any clear meaning, each moment indistinguishable from the next. I hear snippets of conversations between the doctors and my parents, words like "stomach pump" and "toxic levels" that slice through the fog in my mind, but they feel distant, foreign. My father asks questions, his voice calm but strained, and I can hear the tension in his words, though it feels like they come from far away. My mother, on the other hand, shuts them down immediately, refusing to entertain the idea.

"You're not putting her through that," my mother snaps one day, her voice sharp, cutting through the haze like a knife. "She's been through enough."

"Without it, the damage could be permanent," the doctor counters. "Her liver—"

"No," my mother interrupts, her tone hard, unyielding. "Find another way."

I hear the conversation as though from underwater, the words distorted and garbled by the thick fog clouding my thoughts. I don't care what they do to me. It doesn't matter anymore. Nothing matters.

My body changes as the days pass, slowly at first, then faster as the poison works its way through me. My skin takes on a sickly yellow hue, my eyes turning the same dull sunflower shade, lifeless and dim. I hear someone, maybe a nurse, murmur something about organ failure, but it doesn't register, the words meaningless and fleeting. My limbs feel like lead, dragging me down into a state of constant heaviness. My head throbs relentlessly, a constant hammering behind my eyes. I drift in and out of consciousness, caught in a limbo where my dreams blend with reality, and it becomes impossible to tell where one ends and the other begins.

I talk to people who aren't there—my brother, the strange boy with dark hair, even Monkey. I tell them things I've never spoken aloud before—my fears, my regrets, my anger. I confess everything, the words spilling from me in a torrent, raw and unfiltered. But when I open my eyes, it's always my mother sitting there, staring at me with a mixture of exhaustion and something else I can't quite place. It feels like pity, perhaps, or maybe just a deep, aching weariness. Either way, it makes me feel more alone than ever.

Eventually, I stop speaking altogether. I'm too afraid to trust my mind, too afraid that I'll say something that will give away just how broken I am. The silence becomes my shield, my way of keeping the world at bay, of preventing anyone from seeing the depth of the darkness consuming me.

I don't know how long I've been in the hospital when a nurse comes in one evening to change my IV. The woman is kind, her voice soft and gentle as she asks how I'm feeling. I don't answer her. I just stare at the ceiling, the sterile white tiles above me spinning in slow motion. My hands clutch the edge of the blanket, my fingers digging into the fabric as if it can ground me, though I know it won't.

"You're going to be okay," the nurse says, her tone full of that false reassurance I've heard so many times. "It'll take time, but you'll get through this."

I want to believe her. I want to believe that there's a way out of the darkness, that this isn't the end. But as I lie here, my body weak and poisoned, my mind trapped in a fog, I don't know if I can. The words don't comfort me; they only make the weight of it all feel heavier. I'm so tired. Too tired to even fight for a way out.

The Promise

The day I leave the hospital is bleak, overcast, and cold. The sky is a heavy grey, like a thick blanket pressing down on everything, and the wind cuts through the air, biting at my skin as I step through the automatic doors. My legs are weak and unsteady beneath me, like they no longer belong to me, and I take each step slowly, trying to hold myself together. The wheelchair they insisted I use to get to the car sits abandoned just inside the building, its cold, sterile wheels gleaming under the harsh fluorescent lights, and I'm grateful to leave it behind. I don't want another reminder of how helpless I've become. The idea of needing assistance, of being cared for in that way, feels like a humiliating betrayal of who I thought I was.

My mother walks ahead of me, her pace brisk and purposeful, like she has somewhere to go, someone to be with—someone who is *not* me. She speaks in clipped tones to my father, who trails behind her, carrying my things in silence. His face is unreadable, his jaw clenched as though he's trying to hold back a storm, but it doesn't matter. The words they exchange are muted and distant, as though I'm not there. Their conversation is a low murmur, like background noise to a scene in a film, but I can't make sense of the dialogue.

I feel like a ghost, floating through the motions of a life that no longer feels like my own. Everything is out of focus, and the edges of reality seem blurred, as though I'm detached, watching from a distance. But beneath the numbness is anger, hot and sharp, simmering just beneath the surface, threatening to spill over. It's a fire that's been burning for so long that I don't even remember the last time I felt calm, safe, or in control.

I wanted this to be over. I was so sure it would be. The certainty had settled deep inside me like a lead weight, pressing down on my chest, making it hard to breathe. I can't shake the memory of the pills in my hand, their cold plastic bottles slick with sweat, and the heavy certainty that taking them was the right choice. It was meant to be an escape, a way out, a final release. The second container had been my insurance, my way of ensuring there would be no coming back. No mistakes, no second chances, no saving me this time.

And yet, here I am, alive. Still here. Still stuck. Every breath feels like a betrayal, and I don't know how to move forward when it feels like the life I left behind is already gone.

The car ride home is silent. My mother stares straight ahead, her eyes fixed on the road, her face drawn and tight, her knuckles white as she grips the steering wheel. My father sits next to her, his hands clasped in his lap, his gaze fixed out the window as if pretending the world outside might make sense of the silence between us. I sit in the back seat, staring at my hands, the emptiness of my thoughts mirrored in the clenched fists resting on my lap. My stomach churns with a mixture of anger and shame, the kind that feels like a lump in my throat that I can't swallow. I feel like I'm suffocating, the weight of their unspoken words pressing down on me like a physical force, suffocating me in a way that the hospital bed never did.

When they finally pull into the driveway, I don't wait for them to say anything. I don't need their empty apologies or reassurances. I get out of the car and walk inside, heading straight for my room. The door clicks shut behind me, the sound almost final, and I stand there for a moment, my chest heaving with emotion I don't know how to process, my hands clenched into fists. The quiet in my room is a relief, but it also feels like a trap. My thoughts are louder now that there's no-one to distract me.

I want to scream, to tear the room apart, to do something, anything, to release the rage building inside me. Instead, I sink onto the edge of my bed, my fingers gripping the fabric of my blanket so tightly my knuckles turn white. The fabric feels like the only thing anchoring me to this world, even as the rest of my life seems to be slipping away.

The days that follow are a blur. My parents barely speak to me, their avoidance almost comical in its transparency. The tension in the house hangs thick in the air, a cloud of dread that we all tiptoe around. The only conversation they have about what happened takes place two nights after I'm home. It happens in the kitchen, late in the evening, when the house is quiet, and the air is thick with unspoken tension. The silence presses against my eardrums as if the walls themselves are waiting to see what will happen next.

My mother sits at the table, her arms crossed over her chest, her posture rigid as though she's bracing herself for something. Her eyes are dark and distant, staring at the surface in front of her as if it might hold the answers. My father stands by the counter, his face lined with worry, the sharp angles of his features making him look older, like time itself is taking a toll on him. I lean against the doorway, my arms wrapped around myself, waiting for whatever lecture or interrogation they've been building up to. The air is so thick with tension that I feel like I can hardly breathe.

My mother clears her throat, her gaze fixed on the table. "Was it the letter?" she asks, her tone flat, devoid of emotion. The question hangs in the air, sharp and accusing, like a judgment waiting to be delivered.

I blink, confused for a moment. "What letter?" I ask, though my voice is hollow, the words coming out automatically like I'm not speaking at all.

"The one from your biological mother," she says, her voice growing sharper, the accusation lacing her words. "The one you destroyed."

I freeze, my mind racing. I remember the letter, the single sheet of paper that had been kept in a box in my parents' room. I had torn it into pieces the moment I overheard the conversation between my mother and brother that one time, the weight of the anger and hurt unbearable. It felt like I was being suffocated, trapped in a life that didn't belong to me. I tore it up to stop it from haunting me, from reminding me of a truth I wasn't ready to face.

"That's what this was about, wasn't it?" my mother continues, her eyes narrowing. "You were upset about that letter."

I stare at her, disbelief coursing through my veins, the anger bubbling up in waves. "No," I say, my voice trembling with rage. "This wasn't about the letter."

"Then what?" she demands, her voice rising, the desperation creeping into her tone. "What could make you do something like that?"

I want to scream, to shout the truth at her, to lay bare all the years of pain and humiliation and rage I've carried. I want to tell her that she's the reason, that it's her cutting words and cold glares, her impossible standards and constant disapproval, which drove me to the edge. But I don't. I can't. Because I know she won't hear me. She never has. Her mind is made up, and no amount of words can change that.

Instead, I clench my fists at my sides, my nails digging into my palms. "You wouldn't understand," I say, my voice cold and flat, the words falling from my mouth like stones.

My mother scoffs, shaking her head. "Of course, I wouldn't. You've made sure of that."

I bite the inside of my cheek so hard I taste blood, the pain sharp enough to ground me, to stop the storm that's threatening to consume me. I don't respond. I turn on my heel and leave the room, my heart pounding in my chest, my every step a rejection of everything she represents.

Later that night, my mother came to my room. I'm sitting on the bed, staring at the wall, my mind racing with thoughts I can't seem to control, a whirlpool of confusion and anger threatening to drag me under. My mother doesn't knock; she never does. She steps inside, her arms crossed over her chest, her expression unreadable, as if she's trying to mask something—guilt, perhaps, or fear.

"You need to promise me something," she says, her voice firm, her tone unmistakably authoritative.

I don't respond, don't look at her. I don't want to look at her.

"Promise me you'll never do that again," she continues. "No more pills, no more... whatever that was. You hear me?"

I glance at her, my jaw tight, the promise heavy in my chest. "Fine," I say, my voice hollow, like I'm speaking from a distance. "I promise."

My mother studies me for a moment, as though trying to decide if she believes me. Then she nods and leaves the room, shutting the door behind her with a quiet click.

I exhale shakily, my hands trembling as I press them to my face. The promise feels like a shackle, tightening around my chest with every passing second. I know the promise means nothing. It is a lie; a flimsy agreement made to get her out of my room, to calm her. Because I know, deep in my heart, that if I ever get the chance again, I will not fail. I will not make the same mistakes. I will not leave it up to chance.

My mother thinks the letter is the reason, a convenient scapegoat for what happened. But I know the truth. It is she who broke me, piece by piece, over the years. It is she who made me feel like I was unlovable, a burden, a mistake.

And yet, as I lie awake in the dark, the weight of my promise pressing down on me like a shackle, I wonder if I will ever have the courage to tell her the truth. Or if it even matters anymore.

On the Threshold of Quiet Comfort

Whenever I go to see my Mistress, I keep an open mind, knowing that each session offers something different. There's usually a two-week gap between our meetings, and during that time I process countless thoughts, memories, and emotions. Each passing day builds a quiet tension within me, a kind of internal stirring that only gets resolved when I return to her. By the time I walk into her space again, I am both restless and eager, ready for the release she offers—a deep, cleansing reset for both my body and mind, a kind of shedding that feels almost sacred.

By now I've developed a strong preference for the bench and the caning that comes with it. It's raw, unrelenting—a reminder of my pulse, my breath, my body. It is a truth I can feel in every nerve, a raw experience that roots me in the moment. The sting of each strike has a rhythm to it, a dance between pain and relief. Yet, there is also something uniquely powerful about OTK sessions. They feel like an act of profound kindness toward myself, a delicate dance of trust and submission. The experience is almost meditative. I surrender, and in that surrender, there is something quiet and healing. The soft pressure of her lap against my body feels grounding, almost like an anchor. Sometimes, I think I could spend an hour simply lying there, feeling my energy settle and my mind finally find stillness. That space between us has become a sanctuary of sorts, a place where I am safe enough to let go, where I can feel both held and free at the same time.

In the beginning, I was acutely aware of how exposed I was in front of her, and how she saw me at my most vulnerable. It felt like standing stripped and bare, every fragile part of me laid open for her to see. But she never judged me—not once. No matter how little I shared, no matter how fragmented my words or feelings were, there was never any harshness or disgust in her eyes. Her gaze was always steady and kind, even when I wasn't kind to myself. Her presence was both grounding and gentle, a steady force that allowed me to be myself—imperfect, messy, and raw.

I remember the first time she pulled me over her lap. It was the day after my birthday—a day that has always carried emotional weight for me. Birthdays remind me of something I was never meant to be, of the love I never received, of the absence that lingers in the spaces of my heart. That particular year, my mother didn't call or message me. I told myself I didn't care, but beneath that indifference, a quiet sting of abandonment remained. It was a reminder that in her eyes I had never truly mattered.

That day, my Mistress gave me a session unlike any before—a deeper, more intense one, filled with purpose. It was exactly what I needed. By the end, I felt raw, spent, and emotionally stripped. But there was a quiet relief in the release, something that let me breathe again, if only for a moment.

And then, in that soft pause after the storm, she asked, "Would you like a hug?"

At first, I wasn't sure if I had heard her correctly. The question seemed foreign, almost fragile, in contrast to the harshness of the session we'd just completed. My instincts screamed at me to say no, to deny the weakness that seemed to rise in my chest. To put up walls, to shut down, to walk away as I had always done. These were the reactions that had protected me for years, the armour that had kept me safe from feeling too much, from trusting too much.

But I looked at her, perhaps longer than I should have, and I realised with a mix of confusion and longing that I wanted a hug. No—more than that, I needed one.

Quietly, almost in a whisper, I heard myself say, "Yes."

And without hesitation, she just held me. There was no rush, no awkwardness—just the soft pressure of her arms around me, offering comfort in a way I had never fully allowed myself to receive. In that embrace, I could feel something in me begin to shift. The weight that had been so heavy on my chest, the tension I had carried for so long, began to loosen. It wasn't a cure, but it was a balm, and for the first time in a long while, I felt something close to peace. It was as though I had let go of an old wound that had never truly healed, and in its place something new was beginning to form—a fragile sense of trust, perhaps, or the beginnings of self-compassion.

Starting Over

The failed suicide attempt hung over me like a heavy, unshakable burden, one that felt almost impossible to recover from. It was as though the air around me had thickened, a suffocating presence that everyone could feel but no-one dared to address. The silence was deafening. No-one asked how I was doing or whether I was okay. It was as if I had become invisible, as though my pain was something too uncomfortable to acknowledge. I was left to grapple with it alone, to process in isolation the weight of my actions and the emotions that followed.

I could also sense a shift in my brother's behaviour. He, too, seemed to carry an invisible weight, a heaviness that clung to him in ways I couldn't explain. There was a subtle tension in the way he moved, in the way he looked at me. I sensed guilt lingering beneath the surface, though I never blamed him. After all, he wasn't the cause of my turmoil. He was just another voice on the outside, repeating the same things I had already played over in my mind. His well-meaning but detached comments, though intended to comfort, only deepened the silence. They made the quiet feel even louder, like a pressure I couldn't escape. And instead of feeling understood, I felt more distant from everyone around me. The words, though caring, seemed hollow, as though they couldn't bridge the gap between the way I felt and the way others perceived me. It was as if we were all caught in a moment, unable to move past it, each of us unsure how to break the stillness that hung in the air.

My parents, instead of offering any kind of support or even asking if I needed help, simply told me not to talk about what had happened. As though I would ever want to make it public knowledge. I didn't argue, though the anger and shame that swelled inside of me were almost too much to bear. I felt the weight of their silence like a physical force, pressing down on me, making it harder to breathe. But when they added that they would keep it a secret for the sake of the family, because they feared people might wrongly attribute the incident to the fact that I was adopted, it hit me harder than I ever expected. The pain of their words cut through me like a knife, revealing just how little they truly understood. That moment crystallised a painful truth: they saw me through a lens of stereotypes and misunderstandings, unable to grasp the complexities of my experiences. It was another stark reminder that, despite all the years we had spent together, we were fundamentally different in ways they couldn't even begin to comprehend or, perhaps, acknowledge.

I often find myself wondering if they ever considered how lucky they were to have been able to raise children, especially since my mother had struggled with infertility.

The next two years were a blur of survival, a chaotic blend of routine and uncertainty that left little room for anything else. Time seemed to pass in fits and starts, each day blending into the next, as though I were simply going through the motions without ever really living.

One afternoon, we met with my mother's friend Judy, whom she had known for years. She shared stories about her daughter's experience in America, how she had spent a year as an au pair, living abroad, learning new things, and expanding her world. Her words sparked something in me, a flicker of hope that hadn't been there for a long time.

Somehow, despite my reservations, my mother agreed that this kind of experience could be beneficial for me—an opportunity to break free from the stifling, familiar world I had known. And so, from that day forward, signing up became my new purpose. It wasn't just a goal; it became the focal point of my life. Each step I took toward making it happen gave me something to focus on, a reason to get through the gruelling, monotonous days ahead. I told myself, *I can do this. I have to do this.* There was no other choice.

Freedom felt so close, so tangible, like something I could almost touch. But it was never about the kind of freedom most people think of—the freedom to go wherever I pleased or do whatever I wanted. The freedom I craved, the freedom that had eluded me for so long, was a mental liberation. And in those fleeting moments when I allowed myself to imagine what it would feel like, I knew I could survive the next two years if only to reach that elusive peace.

Enduring those years, though, wasn't easy. It wasn't a simple matter of grit or resilience; it was a continuous battle, both internal and external. You would think that after nearly losing a child—after being granted the rare and precious gift of a second chance—my parents might have used that opportunity to reflect, to understand the deep cracks in their own lives and their parenting. They could have acknowledged their mistakes, and their flaws, and learned from them. But instead, they remained unchanged. They continued as they always had, stubbornly resisting the possibility of growth or improvement. It was as though they couldn't see that there was something more to be gained from their experiences than just survival. And so, I was left to figure out the meaning of my existence, adrift in a sea of uncertainty, without any real guidance or support.

When my brother found a job and moved out, the loss hit me like a physical blow. Despite the endless arguments, the disagreements, and the distance that had grown between us over the years, his absence left a void that was hard to fill. I hadn't realised how much I had relied on his presence, how much his voice had been a constant, even if it was sometimes a source of frustration. When he was gone, it was like the world had shifted in a way I couldn't quite grasp. His absence wasn't just a change in the house—it was a change in me. I felt a deep, almost unbearable sense of loss. My loneliness intensified, and I found myself grappling with it in silence, without knowing how to make sense of it.

School, once a place where I could hide in plain sight, no longer felt important to me. The first term after he left, I barely cared about grades, assignments, or the teachers' lectures. I stopped pretending to be interested in anything beyond the bare minimum. It was as though I had buried my head in the sand, trying to avoid facing the reality of my feelings, trying to escape the overwhelming emptiness that threatened to consume me. My report card reflected my disinterest, my grades slipping, and my effort waning. But by the second term, something shifted in me. Slowly, I pulled myself together. I forced myself to engage again, to focus on something, anything, that could help me feel like I wasn't drowning. I threw myself into sports, into extracurricular activities, hoping that by keeping my body busy, I could find some release for the emotional turmoil that still swirled beneath the surface. It wasn't a solution, not really, but it was a way to survive. And for now, that was enough.

As I grew older, the complexities of relationships became more apparent, like a tangled web that I struggled to navigate. I began to feel the stirrings of attraction toward boys but quickly realised that my connections with them were often confusing and filled with tension. Perhaps it was because I was a complex person—someone whose mind worked in layers, whose emotions were more fluid and unpredictable than I cared to admit.

I loved the rush of falling in love—the butterflies in my stomach, the heady excitement, the sense of endless possibilities. It was exhilarating, like I was on the edge of discovering something new about myself with every moment. But when things began to shift—when someone expected more, when they wanted commitment—I felt a weight settle on me. The idea of belonging to someone, of being expected to conform to their needs and desires, seemed impossible. The thought of being someone's property, of being confined to a set of rules and obligations, felt suffocating. I wanted freedom, not a cage built from someone else's expectations.

The neediness, the constant demands, the emotional pull—they all became suffocating, like being wrapped in a blanket that was too tight, cutting off my breath. I needed space to breathe, to think, to remain the person I was without being altered by someone else's wants. And so, when things inevitably ended, I was brutally honest. There were no sugar-coated words, no vague excuses. I would tell them exactly what I was feeling, no pretences, no games. *Why can't it just stay casual?* I would ask myself. But more often, I'd ask them, trying to understand why things couldn't stay simple. It was as if I craved the carefree, the light-heartedness that relationships often promised but rarely delivered. And even when I set boundaries, even when I tried to keep things straightforward, things never stayed uncomplicated for long. It wasn't long before I found myself once again needing to explain why it wasn't going to work out, defending my decision, and justifying my need for space.

I became *extremely* picky—perhaps more than was fair. It wasn't just about the big things; it was about the little things, too. If someone couldn't kiss well, if there was even the slightest hint of poor personal hygiene, I didn't hesitate to walk away. It wasn't a matter of being judgmental; it was about protecting my standards. A dealbreaker was a dealbreaker, and I had no tolerance for mediocrity in relationships. I wasn't interested in settling for someone who couldn't match my energy or meet my expectations—however high they may have been.

I didn't play games. I wasn't the type to indulge in petty jealousy or thrive on drama, those things that seemed to consume so many teenage relationships. It felt pointless, almost juvenile, to worry about who was talking to whom or who liked whom more. My resilience made it easy for me to walk away without hesitation, without second-guessing myself. I didn't need anyone to complete me, because I was already whole. I didn't need their emotional baggage, their unresolved issues, their constant demands. I was content in my own company, and comfortable with the space I created for myself. Relationships, for me, were not about dependence or ownership. They were about connection, mutual respect, and freedom—qualities that seemed to be in short supply the deeper I ventured into the world of romantic entanglements.

At seventeen, I entered into a brief, yet memorable, fling with my driving instructor, who was thirty at the time. The arrangement suited me perfectly. We could meet up without the baggage or emotional demands that came with relationships in high school. There was an undeniable thrill to it, especially because we both knew it was forbidden. He was older, in a committed relationship, and, most notably, he was a man of colour. If my parents had known, they would have been furious. My mother suspected something, but I always managed to deny it, hiding the truth behind carefully crafted excuses.

At times, I found myself juggling more than one person, each relationship in its bubble of complexity. It was exhilarating at first, the excitement of keeping things fresh, but it quickly became overwhelming. I was terrible at keeping up with the lies and dealing with the emotional weight of it all. The balance became impossible to maintain, and I couldn't shake the constant anxiety that one of them would find out about the others.

When prom came around, I found myself facing a dilemma. I couldn't decide who to go with, and by then, my list of break-ups was long enough to feel like a small archive of failed attempts at relationships. Still, I was determined not to attend alone. There was someone in the year below me who had caught my eye. He wasn't like the boys in my year. He seemed more mature, like he had a different perspective on life. Something about him spoke to me on a deeper level, though I couldn't quite put my finger on it. It wasn't just physical attraction; there was an energy between us that felt almost fated. I wasn't concerned about what others might think or how they might judge me for my choice. I didn't care if it raised eyebrows. I simply felt that it was right.

I made sure he noticed me. I would catch his gaze during assemblies, holding it just a moment longer than usual. It was subtle but deliberate, a way of signalling that I was paying attention, that this wasn't accidental. I wanted him to know that I was interested and that I was making my move.

One Friday after assembly, I walked up to him, heart pounding in my chest, and asked, "Would you consider joining me for prom?" His response was immediate, and I couldn't contain the rush of relief and excitement that flooded through me. I managed to keep my cool, though inside my heart was racing.

In the months that followed, we spent hours talking, and through our conversations, I learned that he had liked me for years. It felt surreal, almost like fate had brought us together at the right time. In many ways, he became a beacon of light during my final year of school. He was kind and genuine and seemed to have his life together in a way that I admired. We shared so many of the same interests, and even when the relationship eventually turned physical, we both agreed that it wasn't about rushing things—it was about enjoying the experience for what it was. We were open to experimentation, to discovery, and to whatever came next, with no pressure or expectations.

I remember that night after prom so vividly. He couldn't make it to the after-party, for reasons I can't quite recall. But in the blur of the evening, I ended up hooking up with someone else. I don't know why I did it, but the guilt that followed was immediate and overwhelming. It was the first time I had ever felt that way, and it hit me like a ton of bricks. I realised at that moment that I didn't like the person I had become. I had betrayed someone who had been nothing but kind to me, and that feeling made me question everything I thought I knew about myself. He came from a beautiful family— loving parents, a strong sense of purpose, and a clear direction in life. He had so much going for him, and

I couldn't help but think that he deserved better than someone like me, someone who was still figuring things out and who had made mistakes. He was the kind of guy who would do well in life, someone who could make a great partner someday.

But I knew my departure to the U.S. was fast approaching, and I couldn't help but feel a sense of relief. I wanted to leave—leave everything behind. I craved a place where no-one knew my name, where I wasn't tied to my past, my family, or anyone else. A place where I could start fresh, without the weight of memories that had been imprinted on me for so long. Deep down, I had always known that this would be my chance to reinvent myself, to shed the skin I had carried for years. It felt like the beginning of a new life—one that I could shape into something entirely different, something that reflected who I truly was or who I hoped to become.

I was excited, yes, but there was also a quiet undercurrent of uncertainty. The unknown loomed large. I had no idea what awaited me in this new land, what kind of challenges or opportunities I would face. But one thing was clear: I was ready. Ready to leave behind the life I had known and embrace the unfamiliar. My departure wasn't just a physical relocation—it was a symbolic break from everything that had defined me up until that point. It was my opportunity to start anew, to write a different story for myself, one where I could finally be in control. There would be no turning back now. The moment had arrived, and with it, the promise of a future untold.

Ivoryton

The day of my flight was strange, to say the least. All I had ever known was life in South Africa—the culture, the rhythm, the people. Saying goodbye to my parents was more complicated than I had imagined. There were tears, yes, but it wasn't because I was leaving behind my home or my family. It wasn't homesickness that tugged at my heart. It was something deeper—a recognition that this departure was the beginning of an ending, a pivotal moment that marked the start of a new chapter. And that chapter, as much as I had hoped for it, would be one I would have to face alone.

But still, I was ready. I knew that this was the right step for me, even if the road ahead was uncertain. I had always been a survivor, and this would be no different. This new life, no matter how daunting, was a chance to find a version of myself I hadn't yet discovered. A chance to rewrite everything.

When I arrived in Ivoryton—a picturesque village within the town of Essex, Connecticut—I was both relieved and intimidated. I had been placed with a family that seemed perfect on paper. My host mom was a lawyer, my host dad was in the Navy, and they had two girls. I was surprised by the quiet charm of their small town, with its tree-lined streets and idyllic, peaceful atmosphere. It felt like a world so different from everything I had known. I was nervous about living with children, unsure of what that would be like. I had no expectations, no framework for what a family should look like or how I should behave in it. The unfamiliarity of it all only made me feel more like an outsider.

But my host family was amazing. From the very first moment I arrived, I felt a sense of peace wash over me. The house was warm, inviting, and serene—a place that offered solace from the uncertainties of being in a new country. I was very shy at first—barely 18, with no life experience, and I felt every ounce of my youth and inexperience. My host dad, John, had this laid-back demeanour, making him approachable and easy-going in many ways, yet he was also curious and open-minded. His travels had taken him to places far and wide, and his deep respect for new cultures was evident in the way he spoke about his adventures.

Kate, my host mom, was a woman who found joy in the little things. Soft-spoken but resilient, she had a quiet strength and a deep love for reading, often losing herself in novels that spanned a wide range of genres. They never raised their voices, and their calmness was a refreshing contrast to the chaos I had known. Together, they created an environment that felt grounded, generous, and full of warmth.

Kate's parents owned a cherry farm in Michigan, and when we visited them, I felt embraced by the love they radiated. They were the type of grandparents who made you feel cherished in every conversation and gesture.

On the other hand, John's parents were more reserved and a bit more complex, as is often the case with highly intelligent people. Their interactions were thoughtful and sometimes understated, but it was clear they cared deeply for their family.

In the beginning, I mostly wanted to find my footing—settle in, enjoy the comfort of my own space, and savour the tranquillity of a calm, peaceful home. I was drawn to the stillness, a welcome break from the noise of the outside world. No moods, no arguing, no bitterness—just the steady hum of contentment. While the other au pairs often invited me out, eager to include me in social events, I found solace in the quiet moments spent on my own, relishing the peacefulness that came with solitude. I was very aware of not wanting to come across as antisocial or someone who preferred isolation (which, admittedly, I did), so when I was introduced to a woman named Pascal who invited me to her house to play cards, I accepted the invitation as a way to appear like I had plans, to fit in.

Though the invitation seemed a little strange at first, something about Pascal's energy intrigued me. She had a quiet warmth that drew me in, something that made me feel like maybe, just maybe, I wasn't entirely lost. I still remember the Saturday evening I made my way to her farmhouse, wondering why on earth I had agreed to this. But as I neared her house, I felt a sense of calm wash over me. The door opened, and the smile in her eyes mirrored the one on her face—gentle, sincere, and welcoming. There was no overwhelming presence, no loud enthusiasm; she simply seemed like a person who was comfortable in her skin, and I found that deeply reassuring. She didn't demand much from me—not attention, not conversation. It felt as though she could sense I was a little lost, perhaps even carrying some invisible weight, but she never pried. I never shared the details of my childhood with anyone, certainly not that it wasn't the typical, carefree, happy upbringing. It was something I never felt comfortable disclosing, so I kept conversations brief, light, and positive, doing my best to avoid any depth.

Pascal and I would sit at a small wooden table near the warmth of the fireplace, playing cards in quiet companionship. Often, we didn't need words at all. It was as though we both enjoyed each other's company, despite the silence. She didn't probe or ask personal questions; it was as if she could sense I needed the space to compose myself. While the other au pairs would talk about being homesick and missing their parents, I felt something different: fear. I was scared—scared of the sudden weight of responsibility that adulthood seemed to demand. I didn't feel like an adult yet, and the thought of having to manage my own life overwhelmed me. I didn't even know the basics, like how to open a bank account or use a washing machine without fumbling.

Pascal never pressured me. She simply gave me an open invitation: "Come as often as you want, whenever you want," she would say with a calm assurance. And I did. For the first few weeks, I visited her often, seeking solace in her quiet presence. She became a strange comfort during those initial, uncertain days. But as time passed, and I grew more comfortable in my new life, something shifted. Just like that, I stopped going. I was ready—to embrace my youth, to be free, to travel, to meet people. Pascal's house, once a place of refuge, became a memory of a time when I was still learning what it meant to be myself.

In my third month of arrival, I had already formed a close friendship with Kamilla, a girl from Denmark, and Bay, another from Germany. At times, I probably seemed a bit eccentric to them, with this restless energy that surged within me, always pushing me to do more, see more, and experience everything around me. I was fuelled by a spontaneous urge to live life to its fullest—long walks at 4 a.m. to catch the first light of the sunrise, impromptu trips to New York, and weekend road trips to destinations that called to us on a whim. I couldn't get enough of this new world I had stepped into, and I was determined to soak up every moment.

The three of us shared a deep love for nature and the great outdoors, relishing the fresh air and the beauty of the world around us. We had no interest in the typical party scene—no wild nights of clubbing or excessive drinking. Instead, our adventures were filled with quiet moments of reflection, laughter, and a sense of wonder at the simple things. Bay, who lived in the same small town as me, and I spent the most time together.

At first, our interactions were a bit awkward. We both stumbled through the early days of our friendship, unsure of each other. I suppose I chalked it up to her being German, with a different cultural rhythm than mine. And with her being two years older than me, she likely saw me as young and a bit immature. But over time, as we spent more moments together, something stronger began to form between us. A true bond, built on trust and shared experiences, grew steadily as if it had always been meant to be.

There was something about Bay that drew me in—something subtle yet undeniable. It was her calmness, her genuine care, and her unwavering sincerity. She was never one to pretend or put on an act; she was simply herself, and that was enough. She wasn't the fiery, bold type of woman I had always been drawn to in my friendships, but there was an inner strength to her, a quiet resilience that grounded me in a way I hadn't known I needed. In her presence, I felt at ease, like I could let go of the frantic energy I so often carried, and just be.

As time went on, I found myself yearning to share more of my time, my space, and my life with her. It wasn't just a desire—it was a pull, an unspoken need. In her presence, I felt a sense of peace, a comfort that wrapped around me like a warm blanket on a cold night. It was something I had never truly experienced before, a connection so deep that it defied explanation. We didn't need words to fill the silence between us. It was as if we could communicate through a glance, a smile, or a touch. In the nine months we spent together in the U.S., through all the adventures, laughter, and countless memories, it was as though we became two halves of the same whole—soulmates. We had become so intertwined that the thought of being apart was unfathomable.

Since Bay had arrived before me, the time came for her to return home three months earlier than mine. As that inevitable day loomed closer, the weight of it settled into both of our hearts, a constant, aching presence. The days leading up to her departure were unbearable, each passing hour feeling like a slow, torturous countdown. It was heartbreaking, soul-crushing—the kind of pain that seemed to seep into every fibre of your being. We both felt it, deep within our bones, as if the universe itself was conspiring to tear us apart.

In the evenings after work, I would go to her place. We would watch movies, but the scenes on the screen often felt distant, like a faint distraction from the heaviness that hung in the air. The silence between us wasn't uncomfortable—it was both comforting and unbearably heavy, filled with the quiet understanding that our time was slipping away, moment by moment.

We would just lie there, side by side, wrapped in the warmth of each other's company. It wasn't strange—it felt necessary, like an anchor to hold us steady in the face of the sadness that loomed over us. There was something sacred about those moments, a kind of stillness that seemed to say everything we couldn't. I couldn't explain it, couldn't articulate what I felt in my heart—it didn't make sense to me. All I knew was that saying goodbye felt impossible.

Then the day arrived when she had to leave. The air around us felt thick and heavy, as if it had turned to stone. It was suffocating, pressing down on me, making it hard to breathe. My chest tightened, and my body seemed to go numb, as if all the life had been drained from me in one cruel sweep. She felt it, too, I could see it in her eyes—the same emptiness, the same weight bearing down on us. We couldn't find the words to explain it, couldn't even begin to articulate the depth of what we were feeling. We didn't speak. We just stood there, holding each other, our bodies pressed close, letting the silence do what our voices could not. In that stillness, everything was understood.

She gave me one of her shirts, soft and worn, still soaked in the scent of her perfume. It was a small gesture, but it felt like an attempt to soothe the ache that now gripped my heart, a way for her to leave a piece of herself behind. As I held it in my hands, it became a lifeline, a tangible reminder of her presence. It was something to hold onto as I tried, in vain, to comprehend the vast emptiness that had suddenly descended upon me, a space so large it seemed impossible to fill.

And then, she was gone. Just like that, my world shattered.

Everything I had known, everything I had come to love about this country—the quiet mornings, the spontaneous adventures, the laughter shared between us—suddenly became ordinary, stripped of its colour and life. The world felt dull, empty, devoid of meaning. This was a pain unlike anything I had ever known. It wasn't just the ache of missing her—it was an all-consuming force, a storm that tore through me and left nothing in its wake but devastation. It devoured every part of me: my body, my mind, my soul. If I could describe it, it felt as if my heart had been shattered—not just broken, but torn apart into a million tiny, irreparable pieces, each one too small to ever be mended.

be? The time zone would be more manageable, and it was certainly closer to her. I started saving every penny, each one a step closer to a future I could almost taste. I didn't meticulously plan, but I knew what needed to be done: a visa, a flight, accommodation, and a job waiting for me on the other side. I applied to work on a farm, and by the time I left the U.S., everything was set. It was a strange goodbye. At one point I could envision living here, but that was only because of the experience we shared during those few months.

Next Chapter

I arrived in the UK carrying a massive bag, and everything felt foreign. The air was colder, the people more reserved. I felt out of place, disoriented, and homesick—not for my own home, but for everything that once felt good and safe; for something solid. A small, cramped minibus waited at the terminal to take me to the farm where I was to begin work the following morning. The air felt thick with unfamiliarity. My energy was a tangled mess, too unsettled to even breathe right. I didn't want to be here, but somehow I had to be.

As we drove through the vast countryside, rows of weathered caravans dotted the landscape, young people milling around in groups, their laughter like a distant sound I couldn't connect with. I longed for isolation, for the quiet refuge of a space where I could close a door behind me and just be. My heart ached for the company of one person, just Bay—and it shattered me knowing that I couldn't just email or call her to ease the distance between us.

A few people came to introduce themselves and show me around. They led me to the caravan that would be my new home. It was February, and the cold bit into me, seeping through every layer. The thin fleece blanket

I had brought felt like nothing more than a token gesture against the chill. Shit, I hadn't thought this through. The air in the caravan was thick with the smell of stale dampness, as if the walls had absorbed years of moisture. The mattress, stained in ways that turned my stomach, was a constant reminder that this place had been neglected. There was no heating. I could feel the frost nipping at my bones. It was everything I feared.

My mood deepened, sinking further with each passing moment. Was this my reality now? Had I somehow landed in hell? This wasn't at all what I had imagined. I felt lost, isolated, and utterly miserable. I had to force myself to interact, to be social, but each conversation felt like an effort I couldn't summon. I didn't care how others saw me. The caravan park was filled with South African youngsters, most of them smoking, drinking, and experimenting with drugs. I felt like a stranger in a world that wasn't mine. An outsider, unwanted, out of place. I refused to join in their endless cycle of vices, and it made me instantly unpopular.

The nights were the hardest. I asked for bin bags to cover the mattress, desperate to block out the stains and filth. I layered every item of clothing I owned, but it didn't help. That night, snow began to fall. I watched the silent, frozen world outside, my heart aching with loneliness I couldn't escape. I cried softly, unable to hold back the tears. The cold and the isolation seemed endless.

*

The next day, we were up at 7 a.m.—dressed, fed, and ready for a day of gruelling labour. We were loaded into minibuses and taken to factories, where we spent 12 hours boxing bottles of whipped cream. *Jesus Christ, I thought, what have I signed up for?* The monotony was unbearable. The hours dragged on as I stood, aching, unused to the demands on my body. But I didn't let it show. I overheard a few of the others talking about jobs they'd had before—like slaughtering chickens—and how this job was a dream compared to those. It was as if this was supposed to be easier, more tolerable. I couldn't believe it. I was certain now that I had landed in hell. But still, going home was not an option. Somehow, this was the better of the two choices, so I convinced myself to push through.

I kept to myself during the first few weeks, retreating into my thoughts. Then, one morning, as I was eating breakfast alone, someone brought over a package. I recognised the handwriting instantly—it was Bay's. My heart skipped. It felt as if she had reached across the distance and wrapped me in her warmth. Inside the package was a letter, a long one, describing how she missed me and how she, too, felt lost and lonely. She had packed chocolates and a pillow, trying to comfort me from afar.

I had written her a letter shortly after my arrival, describing the cold, lonely nature of this place. She understood, even from miles away. At that moment, I felt something stir inside me—an electric sense of connection, of being truly seen. Her thoughtfulness made the darkness of this place feel a little more bearable. I knew I had to keep going.

So, I started socialising more, attempting to make some connections, even though I knew they would be fleeting and momentary. I made friends with a few of the girls, and in time, they invited me to stay with them in their caravan. It was a double bed—a situation I never would have entertained in my life—but in that moment, it felt like a small mercy. They had a duvet, pillows, and a heater. For the first time in what felt like forever, I felt warm and was able to get a good night's sleep.

I continued to work in the factories, but the weight of this place began to suffocate me. I needed more money and more opportunities if I ever wanted to break free. Then, one day, an opportunity to earn some extra cash appeared. We were offered the option to work a night shift at a nearby milk factory for extra cash. I heard about the opportunity through one of the guys there and his cousin. It was a complicated situation, as they both seemed to want something more than just friendship from me, but my heart was elsewhere, forever tethered to Bay. Still, I appreciated their kindness and how they looked out for me.

I agreed to the night shift, not fully understanding what it entailed. The smell in the factory was unbearable. It clung to everything. I wanted to vomit, but I pushed through. It was hard work—heavy buckets, the stench, my exhausted body protesting with each step. But I didn't ask for help. I didn't complain. One of the guys noticed, though, and quietly took on my load so I wouldn't miss out on the money. I felt an overwhelming sense of gratitude toward them that night, despite feeling weak.

The next day, I decided to join the others around the big fire, even though I was still the only one who didn't partake in drinking or drugs. I just needed the company— the warmth of people around me. As I listened, I overheard a conversation. A group was planning to leave for a salad factory in Evesham. They paid three times what we were getting here and offered better accommodation. This was my chance. I didn't hesitate, didn't think twice.

"Can I come?" I blurted out.

They exchanged glances, then said, "There's only one spot left, and we're leaving in the morning."

Without a second thought, I replied, "I'm in." I rushed back to the caravan, gathered my things, and didn't look back. I didn't need to say goodbye to anyone except the girls who had shared their warm caravan with me. The people running this place didn't deserve a farewell or thanks. It was a hellhole, a place built on lies. But it wasn't my problem to solve.

*

The next morning couldn't come quickly enough. As the first light of dawn crept through the windows, the sound of taxis arriving outside felt like the promise of freedom. We quickly piled into the vehicles, eager to leave the place behind. It was a massive relief to finally be heading to our next destination—a fresh start, far from the exhausting and soul-crushing environment we had endured.

Arriving at the train station, we lined up to buy our tickets, the crisp air filling our lungs with each breath. The sense of relief grew stronger. We were a good group of people whose personalities complemented each other well, despite some of us having only joined the group at the last minute. Despite our mismatched origins, we all agreed on one thing: we didn't want to spend any more time in the other place. It wasn't just the work; it was everything about it.

The train journey was a welcome break from the hard labour and long hours we had endured in recent weeks. Sitting in the cozy compartments, we exchanged stories, our laughter echoing in the confined space. It was a moment of peace—something rare in the whirlwind of recent days. It felt great to be surrounded by civilisation again, even if it was only to observe the busy, unaware passengers around us, each wrapped in their own lives.

We finally arrived in Evesham, the small town that would be our next stop. The cool morning air greeted us as we stepped off the train. We piled into another taxi, excited yet cautious about what lay ahead. We were supposed to meet someone from the factory who would take us to our new accommodation. The town was small, quaint, and picturesque, with narrow streets and cosy brick houses that exuded old-world charm. It felt like something out of a picture book— quintessentially English.

At the factory, we were met by a staff member who greeted us warmly, and it made all the difference. The friendly reception helped ease some of the tension that had built up over the past few days. I'm not one to feel at ease with the unknown, and after our last experience, I had very low expectations. But this moment of warmth was enough to spark a flicker of hope.

We climbed into a small minibus, and the journey to our new place was brief. Another sigh of relief washed over me—thank goodness, a real house. It had basic comforts—heating, a kitchen, and a bathroom—but at that moment, they felt like luxuries. After days of makeshift living, this was the comfort I had been craving. We had to share a room, though, which wasn't ideal. I enjoy having my own space, a place to retreat to when the world feels overwhelming. But this was a short-term situation, and I couldn't waste too much thought on it. At least I didn't have to share a bed.

We had two days to settle in before the gruelling shifts started. The long hours ahead were daunting, but I had one goal in mind: to save as much money as I could. The plan was to visit Bay in Germany after this stint, so every penny counted. The shifts began at 4 a.m., which meant getting up at 3 a.m. to catch the minibus at 3:30 and working until 4 p.m.—seven days a week. It wasn't my ideal working life, but it was short-term, and I just had to power through.

Working in a salad factory was exhausting. The temperatures were kept at a steady 0 degrees, sometimes even colder, and the chill seemed to seep into my bones. The cold was relentless, and the monotony of the work didn't help. We spent hours at conveyor belts, chopping salad. It wasn't physically demanding, but the lack of mental stimulation made the time drag on. It felt soul-destroying. I couldn't understand how anyone could do this day in and day out.

The people were friendly, though, and I found comfort in that. I became friends with a couple from Greece, travellers like me, who took on these little jobs to fund their journey. They had fascinating stories to share— places they had been, people they had met. Their tales made the hours of chopping feel more bearable, and I found myself looking forward to hearing more about their adventures.

Then there was the line manager. She took her job far too seriously, constantly looking for faults in our work—even when the task was as simple as chopping lettuce. She had an eagle eye for every small mistake, and it was baffling. But she seemed to derive pleasure from micromanaging us. The Greek couple's husband, in particular, didn't take kindly to her behaviour. He often challenged her, showing his disgust at the way she treated us, and this created some comic relief. It was hard not to laugh at the absurdity of it all. Since we were only there for a short time, we enjoyed causing a little stir, though I sympathised with the others who had to put up with her, as this was their primary source of income.

The Greek couple kept me grounded during those long, tedious days. They reminded me of the kind of nurturing figures who always have your back, like loving grandparents watching over you. Their presence made the experience bearable, and strangely, I looked forward to spending time with them, even though we didn't share much beyond work.

During this time, I struggled to get in touch with Bay. The number she had given me was incorrect, and it seemed like every day after work, I would walk to the phone booth, dialling different combinations, hoping to hear her voice. There was no easy way to connect with someone back then—instant messages or emails weren't easily available like it is today—just a reliance on whatever number you had written down. It felt as though I was losing contact with her, and it was heartbreaking.

But in a stroke of luck, Bay had also given me her sister's number. Eventually, I managed to reach her, and that moment of connection was a huge relief. It confirmed that our bond was real—something tangible that could withstand the distance. After a month of silence, I finally had the right number. It was a simple thing, but it meant everything to me. Mobile phones were just becoming popular then, and I immediately invested in one. Back then, we used scratchcard phone cards to make calls, which made it more affordable.

We began planning for me to visit her for Christmas. We kept a countdown calendar, marking off the days, which made the wait feel more bearable. Our conversations revolved around all the things we'd do together once I got there. These plans became my escape from the cold, endless days in the factory. It was like counting down to freedom. As the days passed, the work grew more bearable, knowing an end date was in sight. It felt like being in prison—only this was a sentence I had chosen, and I knew when I would be set free.

*

That Christmas remains one of the most vivid and memorable times I've ever shared with Bay. Her family welcomed me with open arms, their warmth filling every corner of their home. There was a sense of peace in the air—a tranquillity that I hadn't realised I was craving. The atmosphere was calm, yet purposeful, like every action and every word had meaning. Even though I couldn't speak or understand German at the time, it didn't matter. The language barrier didn't hinder my sense of belonging. I simply felt at ease. The comfort of their presence was something I hadn't experienced before, and it felt as though I was exactly where I was meant to be.

From the moment I arrived, I was drawn to her family. It was as if they embodied the ideal of what a family should be—people who genuinely enjoyed each other's company, who treated each other with a level of respect and kindness that was both natural and sincere. The bond they shared was beautiful, and for the first time, I understood what it meant to be part of something greater than myself.

Though my body ached from the exhaustion of my time in the factory, and my mind yearned for rest, I couldn't bear the thought of missing a single moment with Bay. I wanted to drink in every second of our time together. Back then, we didn't have a word for what we shared—not yet. It wasn't physical, not yet at least, and it wasn't about lust. But even in its quietest form, there was something between us—something deeper than just connection. It was as if her energy, her essence, had woven itself with mine, and I couldn't imagine a life without it.

Nights were the hardest to wait for. I would find myself wishing for the moments when it was just the two of us, alone in the dark. I remember the intimacy of those quiet nights, lying together in the stillness, our bodies close, our minds connected. We would trace the outlines of each other's hands, fingers brushing gently, as soft music played in the background. I could feel the pull of her presence—not just in the physical sense, but in a way that went beyond touch. Sometimes, I would offer to massage her—a gesture that seemed innocent yet stirred something in me. It was something I couldn't quite understand or put into words.

I had been with men before, but it had always been about lust—a simple, physical urge that I needed them to satisfy. And once that was done, I would walk away without a second thought, without expecting anything more. I kept my distance, never allowing myself to get too attached. I never let anyone into my space—not in the way Bay had begun to. There were no sleepovers, no staying over after the night ended. I preferred to leave in the middle of the night, often leaving without a word. It was a way to protect myself, to keep my emotions at bay. My space was sacred to me. I didn't want to deal with the mess of someone else's expectations or the drama that came with asking someone to leave. Maybe I was cold in that regard, but I was okay with it. I owned that part of myself.

But with Bay, it was different. There was no urge to run away. I wanted to share my space with her. I wanted to wake up next to her, to see her face first thing in the morning, to feel her arms around me. The idea of waking up to her smile, to the quiet comfort of her presence, was thrilling in a way I had never experienced before. It was new, and yet it felt natural. I had never imagined myself with another woman, never considered the possibility that I might be gay. I hadn't grown up thinking I was anything other than straight. But this connection—it was something beyond what I could have expected. It was an energy I couldn't explain, a pull that felt like something I had only dreamed of during the many nights spent alone, back in my own home.

I had always known that I couldn't be with someone who would constantly argue, who would throw harsh words at me like daggers. I didn't want that kind of relationship. I wanted something that grounded me; something that made me feel like I could grow, not shrink. With Bay, I felt that. She made me want to be better. For her. For myself. But for now, all I could do was revel in those quiet, peaceful nights together, feeling the connection grow, even as it was still unnamed. It was a feeling that I wanted to hold onto, not yet ready to understand it, but knowing in my heart that it was something worth cherishing.

*

As always, time with Bay seemed to fly by, and before we knew it, we were standing at the airport for yet another painful goodbye. The reality of leaving her and returning to the UK was hard to accept. After spending such a beautiful Christmas with her family, it felt like I was leaving a piece of myself behind. The farewell was always the hardest part for both of us. Every time we said goodbye, it felt like the end of the world. We would hold each other for what felt like an eternity, tears streaming down our cheeks, oblivious to anyone around us. Nothing else mattered but that moment.

The flight back to the UK was a blur, my heart breaking all over again. By the time my plane touched down, the sky was a dull grey, and the rain soaked the world outside. The train ride back to Evesham mirrored my mood, matching the dreariness perfectly. The next day at the factory, the reality hit me—I couldn't do it anymore. I couldn't stay here. I needed to get out. It was a simple yet urgent realisation that I had to find something else.

Someone at the factory mentioned that some hotels were looking for staff, and I jumped at the opportunity. I was fortunate that the first hotel I called needed someone to start right away. Without hesitation, I used the last of my money for a train ticket to Reading, where I would be staying at a hotel on the outskirts.

The accommodation wasn't bad—staff housing with all meals included, which was a welcome relief after the exhausting conditions I had left behind. I was assigned a job as a waitress in the restaurant, a significant improvement over the soul-crushing monotony of factory work. But while it was a step up, serving people wasn't something I felt passionate about. It wasn't my dream job, but it was a means to something better.

Still, the company made all the difference. I worked alongside other young people, and their energy and camaraderie transformed the experience. For the first time in what felt like forever, I had two days off a week. It was incredible. It felt like true freedom—something I hadn't known in so long. During our free time, we hung out, listened to music, or simply socialised. Life felt lighter, like I could finally breathe again, as if a weight I hadn't realised I was carrying had been lifted.

For the first time in a long while, I had more time to truly enjoy myself—to live in the moment. I wasn't just working to survive anymore. I spent hours learning to play the guitar, thanks to a guy named Brandon from New Zealand, who patiently taught me. With all this newfound free time, I finally started to focus on something that made me feel alive, something that gave me a sense of purpose beyond the daily grind. Life became about more than just making ends meet—it was about saving for the next adventure. Bay and I began planning a road trip to Italy for the summer.

That summer, I flew to Germany, and together we rented a car and set off for Italy. The freedom of it all, the spontaneity—we didn't plan much, which was exactly how I liked it. It felt like we were writing our own story, with no restrictions, no limits.

We drove, we stopped, we camped, we slept in the car. It didn't matter where we were; the important part was that we were together.

Venice stands out in my mind as one of the most magical moments of that trip. We wandered through the charming streets, basking in the warm glow of the late afternoon sun and soaking in the vibrant, buzzing atmosphere around us. As we walked, a deep, overwhelming desire to express what I had been feeling for so long took hold of me.

I reached for her hand, wanting her to know it wasn't an accident, that it meant something. I held her gaze, half-expecting her to pull away, but she didn't. Her eyes met mine with the same understanding, the same intensity. It felt like a silent promise passed between us, something that didn't need words. At that moment, I knew—I was hers, and she was mine, in a way that couldn't be explained but was unmistakable.

Returning to the hotel after that summer felt like a heavy weight settling on my chest. The separation from Bay was harder than ever, and my friends could see it. They didn't ask questions, though—most of them never did. I've always been a bit of a dark horse, someone who keeps things close to the chest. Even with my friends, I rarely shared the details of my life, preferring to keep the more vulnerable parts of myself hidden. But they made it easier. Their positive energy kept me from sinking too deep into my thoughts. As the Christmas season approached, the hotel grew busier. We worked late into the night, preparing for the influx of guests. When the work was done, we'd spend the evenings partying, often staying up until 3 or 4 in the morning. There was a sense of living in the moment, of seizing whatever joy I could find in the chaos.

That Christmas, I was determined to spend it with Bay again. I couldn't wait to have two whole weeks with her. Our time together was always filled with magic, the familiarity of the celebrations providing a sense of warmth and belonging. This year, however, felt even more special—there was no question in anyone's mind that what Bay and I shared was something more than a typical friendship. But no-one asked; no-one questioned us. It was as if they could see we were navigating something entirely new, something we weren't ready to put into words.

Returning to the hotel after Christmas was tough. Some of my friends had left to follow their paths—Brandon, for example, had met someone and followed her to South Africa. New people had joined, but it wasn't the same. I grew closer to one of the chefs, and we spent time together, chatting and hanging out. It's funny how the right people can change the atmosphere of a place.

Then, one day, I managed to convince the new manager to let Bay come work at the hotel for a few months. Her presence made everything better, especially with the constant turnover of people. Bay and I would call each other every day. It had been like that for as long as I could remember, but now, I needed to know where we stood.

I decided to test her feelings for me. What we had was wonderful, but I couldn't ignore the fact that I had deeper feelings for her. I wanted more than friendship, and I needed to know if she felt the same.

So, one evening, I called her and said, "The next time I see you, I want to kiss you." I could hear both excitement and nervousness in her voice, but I needed to be certain she understood what I meant. And she did.

When it was time for her to join me, I took some time off work and planned a few days in London for us. I couldn't contain my excitement—it felt like being a child on Christmas Eve all over again, full of anticipation and wonder.

When I met her at the airport, I felt like I was floating. We spent the day in London, just enjoying each other's company. And that evening, back at the hotel, I finally kissed her. It was everything I had imagined and more. It was electric, like a spark igniting something deep within me. My blood ran hot and cold all at once, and in that moment, I felt more alive than I ever had before.

That night, we made love for the first time. It was unlike anything I had ever experienced—slower, deeper, more meaningful. I didn't just want it in the moment; I wanted it always. And in that moment, I knew. This was the person I needed more than anything in my life. I was in love for the first time.

Control

Despite my Mistress being the dominant force in our sessions, there's an undeniable sense of control that I, too, hold—an unexpected, quiet authority, even in my submissive role. These sessions are not just about yielding or surrendering for me; they are about self-mastery. They are about holding onto myself, and maintaining my composure, even when every fibre of my being is crying out to be shattered. It's a paradox, difficult to explain to anyone who hasn't experienced it firsthand, but only a select few are allowed into this fragile, sacred space within my mind—the one where my truest vulnerability lies. Trust, in this context, isn't something I offer lightly. Few people—if any—could offer the kind of leadership that earns my full, unguarded surrender. But when I do surrender, I do so with complete, unwavering commitment.

This complex dynamic likely stems from having to rely solely on myself from a young age. Over the years, I've cultivated a firm, unflinching grasp of reality—no sugarcoating, no self-delusion. I value straightforwardness, directness, and brutal honesty. Asking for help has never been an option, especially not from my parents—emotionally or financially. There's something in me that recoils at the thought of being indebted to anyone. That aversion likely originates in my adoption, where I was constantly reminded to be grateful I wasn't left in an orphanage, even though there were moments when I wished I had been. The unspoken demand for eternal gratitude fostered a deep, unrelenting resentment toward the concept of obligation.

Yet, despite all this, the burden of always carrying everything on my shoulders has proven exhausting. It often feels as if there's no-one to help shoulder the weight, no safe place to release it. As I reflect on this now, I think the greatest gift I could ever give my children—besides unconditional love—would be a happy, carefree childhood and a home where they'll always feel safe, always feel welcomed. A place they can turn to when they're in need. This, I consider to be a form of emotional luxury—something I never had, but something I will give to them.

Despite the suffocating weight of responsibility that I carry, I have to admit that I love being in control of my own life. I wouldn't trade this independence for anything. I relish the freedom of making my own decisions, charting my course, and owning my path and my story. I can be selfish, even stubborn at times, and I don't apologise for that. These traits define me, and I own them. They serve me well in the chaos of life.

But in these sessions, everything changes. In this space, I willingly give up my control—not because I am weak or helpless, but because I choose to. It's a choice that requires composure and discipline. I will never ask my Mistress to stop. I will not allow her to see when the pain pushes me to my limits. I don't need to express it aloud. I embrace it fully. I take it all in silence, savouring the intensity. That silence becomes my strength, my armour, my fortress. It is only as long as I remain silent, holding onto my composure, that I remain untouchable. The day she breaks my silence is the day she breaks me.

In these moments, it's difficult to maintain focus, to stay in control of the calm exterior I've worked so hard to cultivate. But with each strike, with every wave of pain that washes over me, I feel it reshaping my thoughts, organising my emotions, sharpening my awareness. I don't need to explain why I crave this or why I need it. In this space, it's already understood without words. She simply gives me what I've asked for—what I need— and that is more than enough. In this sacred space, it is normal. It is acceptable. Her understanding is evident, not only in the way she gives but also in the way I receive. There is no need for further explanation; it's felt, it's lived, it's shared between us.

But what I value most, what strengthens me beyond anything else, is that she never pities me. There is no trace of sympathy in her eyes, no softening of her touch. She never softens. She sees me for exactly who I am, without judgment or mercy, and that is all I could ever ask for. She doesn't need to make it easier for me. She doesn't need to shield me from my vulnerability. In this way, she gives me what I need most: the clarity of being seen for what I truly am. That in itself is a form of freedom.

The Language of Love

The last few months at the hotel seemed to fly by. The days blurred into one another, but the working hours were somehow more enjoyable, especially because I was surrounded by the one person I truly wanted to be with. We shared moments of laughter, of quiet conversations, and of the kind of companionship that made everything feel a little brighter.

One evening, a few people in our group decided to venture into London for a night out. When they returned, the energy didn't dissipate; instead, it lingered, and we found ourselves spending the rest of the evening in a haze, some of us taking ecstasy. Drugs seem to be a common thread in so many social circles, and I've always found it intriguing how some people can indulge and completely transform their personalities, while others seem untouched, maintaining their core selves no matter the substance. It's like they step into an entirely different world, shedding their former skin to reveal something else entirely.

In the midst of all this, one of the girls offered me a tablet. It was the first time I had felt the curiosity to try it, the need to understand what made it such a big deal for so many people. I hesitated, but eventually, I decided to give in. It was unlike anything I had ever experienced.

The drug didn't sweep me away into chaos; instead, it gently unravelled the threads of my mind, like a soft breeze pulling at a loose strand of fabric. My thoughts, usually neat and structured, now floated effortlessly between ideas, each one more expansive than the last. They scattered, yes, but in a way that felt almost intentional, like ripples across a still pond that stretched far beyond the surface. What was once familiar now felt distant, as if I were seeing it through a new lens, one that revealed the subtle layers beneath the obvious.

My mind, which had always been a quiet observer, seemed to open in ways I hadn't anticipated, like a door creaking open to a room I hadn't known existed. In that room, I found not confusion, but clarity—a strange kind of clarity that came not from answers, but from the freedom to ask new questions. I wasn't lost, nor was I anyone else; I was simply more aware of the boundaries I had built around myself, and for the first time, they didn't seem quite so important. Everything around me—my thoughts, the space, the people—had a different weight, a different significance. And I realised, in that quiet shift, that I was still completely myself, only now, I could see more clearly.

I've always been someone who craves new experiences, yet I've always struggled with the idea of consuming drugs. There was something about it that felt foreign, something deep inside me that resisted. But at that moment, I crossed a line, and it felt like I had lost a part of my innocence. It was as if something irreversible had happened—like a part of me was taken that I couldn't get back. I often battle with my conscience in situations like these, that internal tug-of-war between curiosity and caution. But in that moment, there was no hesitation. I had crossed a personal boundary, one I had set for myself, and it was what it was, nothing more, nothing less.

*

My two-year visa was almost up, and the next chapter of my life was fast approaching, looming just beyond the horizon. The uncertainty of what came next hung over me like a cloud, but there was a sense of excitement too, as if the possibilities were endless. I knew I had to make a decision. So, with a mix of anticipation and trepidation, I applied for a one-year study visa in Germany, planning to spend the year in Bavaria with Bay and her cousin's family. The thought of this new adventure filled me with an eager kind of energy. It was the beginning of something big, something that would shift the course of my life.

The season was spring, and the air was alive with warmth, every breath of it invigorating. Flowers painted the landscape with vibrant colours, and the countryside stretched out before me, picturesque and full of life. The hills rolled gently into the distance, dotted with charming villages and expansive fields that seemed to go on forever. I fell in love with Bavaria immediately— the pace of life, the richness of the culture, and, of course, the food. Everywhere I looked, there was something new to discover, a corner to explore, a little detail that made it feel less like a place I was visiting and more like a place I could call home.

Bay's cousin lived just outside of Munich, in a small, peaceful village called Otterfing. From the moment I arrived, I felt as though I had stepped into a world I had always belonged to, a sense of belonging that wrapped itself around me like a warm blanket. Wilhelm, Bay's cousin, was a banker—a steady, practical man, deeply grounded in his work. His wife, Miriam, was the polar opposite—an enthusiastic traveller who ran a small travel agency, her passion for the world beyond visible in the sparkle of her eyes whenever she spoke of her latest adventures. Their two children, Otto, a three-year-old whirlwind of energy, and Anke, a quiet eighteen-month-old with an endless curiosity, filled the house with laughter and chaos. They were a family that radiated warmth and happiness, and it was easy to see how their home had become a haven, a space where love and joy overflowed.

Not far from them lived Bays aunt and uncle, and it was with her aunt, Diet, that I formed a special connection. Diet was a woman of remarkable strength, her vibrant spirit illuminating any room she entered. She was humble and positive; someone who could make you feel like you were the most important person in the world with just a single glance. Diet's hugs were legendary—tight, enveloping, and warm. When she pulled me into her embrace, I felt as though I had known her for a lifetime.

Despite the language barrier—she spoke no English, and I spoke no German—our communication was effortless, rooted in the universal language of kindness and affection. She made me feel loved in a way that I will always treasure. Her husband, Sly, was a quirky, eccentric man, full of amusing stories and unconventional wisdom. They were a remarkable couple—unafraid to live their lives by their own rules, and their zest for freedom was contagious. Their stories of nude holidays, living life with an unapologetic sense of liberation, were so rare and inspiring that I couldn't help but be captivated by their carefree attitude.

The prospect of studying the German language was both exciting and overwhelming. Life as a student brought with it the usual financial struggles, yet I cherished every single moment. The simple act of taking the train or subway to the university felt like an adventure in itself. Each ride served as a reminder that I was a young person forging my own path, stepping into a new chapter of independence. It felt worlds apart from the gruelling factory work I had endured when I first arrived in the UK—a time I often tried not to dwell on.

I had learned early on the true cost of freedom. My parents had offered to pay for my university fees if I returned home—an offer that tugged at my heartstrings. I had always dreamed of university life and earning a degree, but my freedom meant more to me than any piece of paper. So, I chose a different path— one filled with struggles and hardships that I kept hidden from my family. They never knew the full extent of the challenges I faced, nor the soul-crushing jobs I worked just to survive. When I spoke with them, I always painted an idealised picture, never revealing the quiet, weighty struggles that burdened me.

In my language classes, I discovered a community of like-minded learners, each of us striving to master the complexities of German. We were a diverse group, each person bringing their own unique experiences and perspectives. My Afrikaans background helped me with reading and pronunciation, but the concept of gendered articles—masculine, feminine, neuter—was utterly foreign to me. In the beginning, I thought I could just "wing it" during my first exam. But my overconfidence cost me dearly, and I failed spectacularly.

That failure marked a turning point. I realised that I needed to approach this language learning journey differently. I made the bold decision to quit the formal course and learn German on my own terms. My goal became clear: I wanted to speak the language fluently and truly understand the people around me. The nuances of perfect grammar seemed far less important than the ability to communicate effectively.

So, I threw myself into the language—reading books, watching TV shows, listening to the radio. I sought out every opportunity to immerse myself in German. It wasn't always easy, particularly after long days of self-study. There were times when I felt overwhelmed, when the weight of the task seemed unconquerable. But I found inspiration in the dedication of Bay's cousin, who refused to speak English with me, even when I begged him. His determination to help me succeed was humbling and motivating. Even when I felt like giving up, his persistence pushed me forward, urging me to keep going despite the frustration.

I'm sure I drove Bay crazy with my endless questions: "How do you say this?" "What did they just say?" "What does this mean?" But my determination only grew stronger.

Then, one morning, something extraordinary happened. As we headed into the city for a matinee—a movie with breakfast—I suddenly had an epiphany. Without thinking, I blurted out, "I understand everything these people are saying!" It was a surreal moment, like a dream unfolding right before my eyes. For the first time in three months, the world around me no longer sounded like a chaotic jumble of unfamiliar words. I could follow conversations with focused attention, and I understood them. No longer did I need translations or explanations. It felt as if I had crossed an invisible threshold, a victory over the fog that had clouded my understanding. It was a triumph of persistence, a testament to pushing through the discomfort and finally finding clarity.

It took another three months to reach the next milestone—to learn how to organise my thoughts into coherent sentences and speak them aloud in a way that made sense. The first time I strung together a sentence properly, it felt like I had unlocked a secret door to communication. I was no longer a passive observer of the language; I had become an active participant. I could speak back, joke with others, and engage in genuine conversations. It was a feeling of immense freedom, of true connection. It was no longer just about learning the language—it was about becoming a part of the story, fully immersed in the world around me.

First Session

"Call me when you arrive, and I will tell you how to find me." That was the first time I heard her voice, and with it, a sense of relief washed over me. Her tone, calm and steady, settled something deep inside me, as though my own internal compass had guided me exactly where I needed to be at this moment in my life.

My heart thuds loudly in my chest as my feet carry me over the gravel path, each step crunching softly underfoot. A black convertible is parked in front of the elegant property, its sleek body gleaming in the sunlight. *A woman with excellent taste in cars*, I think, smiling to myself at the irony of finding myself here, at this moment in time, in this unfamiliar place.

The door opens, and a woman steps out. She's dressed in black, her silhouette commanding attention, with exceptionally high heels that elevate her height and presence. She carries herself with a quiet but undeniable confidence. It's immediately clear that she's no stranger to this world—not in a peculiar or strange way, but as someone who has lived through experiences that have shaped her into the person standing before me. The kind of person who wouldn't entertain nonsense or misdirection.

I step inside, unsure of what to say or do. An awkward silence lingers in the air as I quickly remove my shoes, following her lead as we ascend the stairs. She moves with effortless grace, gliding upward as though those heels are an extension of her. Meanwhile, I struggle to keep up, my breath becoming more laboured as I try to match her pace.

The room we enter is simple—almost sterile—with two chairs positioned on either side, a minimalist design that contrasts with the presence of a striking, kinky-looking bench at the centre. Leather straps dangle from it, casting a shadow of intrigue. She must have caught the fleeting look of surprise on my face because, with a soft, reassuring tone, she says, "Don't be frightened of that; it looks scarier than it is."

And yet, I suddenly feel small, exposed, and inexperienced in the face of her radiating confidence. It's as though she's done this countless times, while I, on the other hand, am out of my depth. Instinctively, I retreat into observation mode, my defences rising as a means of self-preservation. She remains calm, unaffected by my uncertainty, carrying herself with the ease of someone who knows exactly what they're doing.

"Some people are very open, and others prefer not to say much," she says, her voice warm but practical, almost conversational. I try to focus on her words, but my mind races, flooded with competing thoughts. Logic battles emotion, struggling to process and make sense of it all. *Maybe this will be my way*, I think—*show up, go through the motions, and leave quietly*. Simple. Detached.

She continues, explaining the various options, all while subtly observing my reactions. "Most people like to warm up over my knee," she suggests. Her voice is matter-of-fact, but the words send a jolt of confusion through me.

Before I can even fully process what she's said, the word "No" escapes my mouth—sharp, immediate, and without thought. Fear, shock, and embarrassment rush in all at once, colliding in a way that makes me feel like a trapped animal caught between fight and flight. My heart races, my face flushes, but somehow I manage to hold it together. I had come here with an open mind, deliberately avoiding any expectations, yet in this moment, it's painfully clear how unprepared I truly am. In some far corner of my mind, I had always envisioned this as something brutal, something punishing that I might deserve, but nothing had prepared me for this encounter.

We settle on the flogger—a decision that seems to ease the tension slightly. I remove my shirt and trousers, feeling exposed in a way I hadn't anticipated. Then comes the next question, her voice calm but unrelenting:

"Would you like me to restrain you?"

Her words take me completely off guard. *Jesus Christ*, I think, almost laughing at the absurdity of it all. And yet, as though someone else were speaking through me, I hear myself say, "Sure."

A thousand thoughts race through my mind in an instant. If anyone who knows me could see me now— vulnerable, exposed, my back turned to a stranger, hands tied, with my mind spinning in a whirlpool of irrational fears. The absurdity of it all, the quiet chaos that I have willingly invited into my life, is overwhelming.

She begins gently. The first strikes are almost soothing, the sensation an odd mix of discomfort and relief. But then, emotions that I had long buried begin to rise within me. A lump forms in my throat, and for reasons I can't quite understand, my body feels like it's teetering on the edge of something I can't control. *Don't you dare cry*, a voice inside me screams, desperately trying to keep the tears from spilling. And yet, something within me shifts, a wall crumbling that I didn't even realise I had built. I want to run. I want to escape. But I also want to stay.

It's as if she has reached into the deepest parts of me, pulling everything I have hidden and throwing it all in front of me at once. The weight of it is staggering. Her strikes grow harder, faster, sharper, and my body responds—sweat forms on my palms, a knot tightens in my stomach, and my hands tremble. I am physically shaking, caught between the urge to scream, to shout, and the desperate need to stay silent.

After what feels like an eternity, we stop. It's enough—intense, overwhelming. As she unties my hands, I rise slowly, unsteady on my feet, my legs weak and shaky. The emotions surge through me like a freight train, sweeping me up and dragging me back into fight-or-flight mode. The room feels charged with an obvious tension, and my ever-sensitive, empathetic nature kicks in, analysing everything—the silence between us, the subtle shifts in her posture, the barely perceptible expressions on her face. My mind works overtime, trying to pick apart every detail, searching for hidden meaning at every glance.

"You're so hard to read," she says, her gaze steady as she watches me struggle to collect myself.

Her words hit me like a slap. Shit. Does she regret taking me on? Did I piss her off? The self-doubt creeps in fast, and I'm overwhelmed by the need to escape. I fumble through my clothes, dressing in a blur, desperate to leave the room and the heavy emotions that linger in the air. Saying goodbye is a blur. I almost reach out to shake her hand but stop myself. Her arms are folded, her gaze unwavering, and I realise that I have no idea how to navigate this moment. She stands there, unaffected, while I scramble to find my footing. Part of me wants to explain myself, to justify the mess of emotions swirling within me, but I say nothing. I just walk away.

The moment I get into my car, the floodgates open. I break down, sobbing uncontrollably. For the entire 40-minute drive home, the tears come in a relentless rush, as if a dam has burst. The exhaustion clings to me for days, like I've been wrung out, every emotion laid bare and exposed. Everything I thought I had buried— the pain, the fears, the unresolved tension—has surfaced, and I have no choice but to face it.

But one thing is certain: I will go back. Back to that strange room, with its mysterious bench, and the woman who demands honesty and trust without ever needing to speak a word.

Next time, though, I will be ready.

Rock Bottom

I genuinely dreaded the flight back to South Africa. The thought of living here again felt suffocating. I tried to keep an open mind, reminding myself that I wasn't that child anymore—that I had grown, experienced independence, and gained strength. But still, the reservations lingered, like shadows I couldn't shake.

As the plane descended, it felt like time had been paused. I swear, time just stood still here. The air was thick with an unspoken weight. This country, with its undeniable beauty, felt alien to me, as if it were a place I could admire but never truly belong to. It didn't feel like home. It felt like a foreign land.

I landed and met my parents at the arrivals area. The greeting was never warm and fuzzy—there was no embrace, no tears, no welcoming arms. Instead, it was stiff, forced, and distant. The tension between us was palpable, thickening the air around us as we exchanged pleasantries that meant nothing. Even the most basic moments felt loaded with unspoken emotions. The argument about where the car was parked, the back-and-forth on which direction to take—everything felt petty, as though nothing was ever simple. My parents, unable to even pretend civility, spoke past each other, as they always did. My mother, in her usual way, made sure I knew exactly how hard and unfair my dad made her life. It's been my burden to witness year after year, and now it felt heavier than ever.

By the time we barely left the airport, I already felt like a trapped animal. The drive home was mostly in silence, with only the occasional, meaningless small talk that made it worse. Being here, in this place, brought the past crashing back—the memories of how unbearably depressing life had been. The stifling weight of those memories seeped back into every corner of my mind, suffocating the small bits of freedom I had once found.

I've always been someone who is guided by energy—the energy of people and places. And here, the energy was overwhelming. It wasn't the kind of energy that made me feel alive; it was consuming, draining, like quicksand pulling me down. I didn't even know how to settle back in. Everything felt off. I had no friends here. I had no car and no means of escape. I was entirely dependent on them, and I hated it. The first thing I needed was my transport, something that could give me the freedom to leave whenever I felt overwhelmed by this suffocating place.

I accompanied my mom to town a few hours after arriving, not because I wanted to, but because it was one of the few ways to break free, even momentarily. It wasn't about the destination—it was just good to get out of the house.

"You know, I hope we can put the past behind us and give this a real chance," my mom suddenly blurted out, as though it was that simple. "I'll give this a go, and I hope you can, too."

Her words hit me like a punch to the gut. I wasn't prepared for that. I had built walls around myself, fortified them with years of distance, and here she was, trying to tear them down.

"Of course I will," I blurted out in response, but the words felt hollow. In my head, I knew that trust with her was impossible. She was too unpredictable, too unstable. Even something as simple as hugging her had become an impossible feat. I had grown so much further from her than I ever had as a teenager. Time apart had only amplified the pain and resentment I felt. And now, here I was—stuck, once again, in this place I couldn't escape.

I didn't even know how to engage with them anymore. I could feel myself slipping into the person I had to become just to survive here—the person who learned to pretend, to wear a mask that fooled everyone, including myself. It was the person I had come to hate. At that moment, I felt distant, cold, and angry.

In the midst of all this, I focused on one thing: getting a small motorbike and a mobile phone. I had to establish some semblance of independence, even if it was only a small victory. Communication with Bay was the most important thing, but I had to hide my emotions and suppress the real truth from my parents. They could never know about us—they were vehemently against our relationship, and even mentioning it would have been a betrayal of their narrow worldview. So, I kept it secret.

I would make sure to call her when my parents weren't home or when I was out. Anything to make sure they never overheard our conversations. As far as they were concerned, there was nothing between us. When I left, I left her behind. But she was the one thing that kept me grounded. She was the only real thing in my life; the one thing that offered any sense of solace.

My parents felt I needed to start looking for something more concrete and signed me up for an accounting diploma. It was the most boring career path I could have imagined, but it meant time away from home, so I went along with it.

I was back home less than a week when the first cracks began to show, and the monster within my mother poked its head out. I knew it was only a matter of time. The way she spoke to me with such venom and bitterness—nothing had changed. We just couldn't exist together. She couldn't help herself. I tried to steer clear of her as much as possible.

My brother lived next door in the converted garage, and it was a welcome break to have him around. I'd jump at every invite to tag along with him and his friends. He'd just started seeing a girl quite a few years younger than him, and it already seemed serious. She was besotted with him, and to be honest, it was just nice to have company at times.

We all went out one Friday to a bar and consumed way too much tequila, followed by ecstasy. I think my brother and I had our drinks spiked, because we fell incredibly ill. The first time I met his girlfriend was when she helped me while I was in a terrible condition, throwing up in the ladies' restroom. It wasn't ideal. Usually, I want to be left alone when I'm in this state; I'd disappear and make sure no-one ever saw me like this. But at that moment, I appreciated her kindness.

My parents never suspected we consumed alcohol, let alone drugs. We always hid our personal lives well from them. I decided to sleep on the couch in my brother's flat to avoid their judgment and intrusive questions about my state, but I felt like death. I had regrettably promised to accompany my mom the next day on some errands, and it was a massive struggle to try and act as normal as I could, especially since I was still high and hallucinating from the drugs. Fuck, I wasn't in a good place.

It was high summer in South Africa, so on the weekends, I made sure to spend as much time away from home as I could. I enjoyed fishing, being in nature, and just the quiet peace of being in my headspace. It wasn't so much about the fishing itself; it was more of an excuse to get out of the house. I went to a lake outside of town, which, in hindsight, probably wasn't the wisest place for a woman to be alone. I often think I had many guardian angels watching over me, especially considering the reckless things I used to do. In my younger days, I had less regard for safety or my well-being, so I lived on the edge, always inviting danger.

I would spend entire days lying in the sun, tanning—or more accurately, burning—and mostly sleeping. The nights were spent wide awake, pondering my future. I had developed an eating disorder while in Germany, and it took on an addictive path of controlling what I ate—or more accurately, what I didn't eat. I only ate one meal a day—a small plate of steamed vegetables. So, avoiding the usual mealtimes and the arguments about my eating disorder was another reason to stay away from home during those hours.

I remember being at the lake one Saturday when the temperature soared to 35 degrees. I hadn't brought any water, and the thirst that overtook me was crippling. I wasn't sure how I'd make it home. There were signs everywhere warning of malaria-infected water, but that day, I had no choice. I had to drink the water from the lake if I was going to make it. I did, knowing full well I could get seriously ill from it—but by some miracle, I didn't.

That day, I also got a severe sunburn. It was so bad that I had to go to a clinic. My backside was covered in blisters bigger than my hand, and my face was the same. "Come have a look here, this girl fried her backside," one of the nurses called out with a grin, waving the others over. "I mean, it's like she sat on the sun itself!"

The nurses gathered around, trying to stifle their laughter as they surveyed the impressive, albeit unfortunate, sunburn that had turned my rear end into a shade of crimson most people would only see on a lobster. I was mortified, lying there with my backside on full display for everyone to see. I could feel the heat rising in my cheeks, and it wasn't just from the sunburn. The nurses were practically giving me a full-on inspection, like I was some kind of science experiment. Each of them was whispering, trying to hold back chuckles, while I could only wish for a hole to open up in the floor and swallow me up. It ended up being third-degree burns, and I had to avoid sunlight for a while after that. Not my finest moment.

Bay and I spoke every day—she was the only thing that kept me going. I could tell her about my struggles, about my parents, and she understood. It was hard on both of us. Her parents also hoped that the relationship would fizzle out, allowing her to focus entirely on her university degree. They wanted me to be just a forgotten thing of the past. I know they were only trying to protect her, to do what was best. Still, it felt harsh to be the villain in this situation, especially when I was stuck here. I would often tell her to forget about me, to walk away, to find someone else.

Three months in, I felt like the living dead. I didn't see a purpose. It was impossible to make a living here, and I didn't want to be here. One morning, I found myself in a massive argument with my mother. I never raised my voice to her and barely ever spoke back, but on that day, something inside me snapped. I lost it like never before in my life.

The last words I yelled in her face were, "Why did you ever adopt me? You don't love me, you never have. You should never have adopted two kids. You never wanted me." I spat the words out with such venom and anger. I didn't even recognise myself in that moment.

I grabbed the keys to my motorbike and left the house. I headed off—anywhere, nowhere—but I drove as if I had the devil inside me, possessed. I didn't care if I crashed; in fact, I almost wished for it, invited it. I screamed into my helmet, tears streaming down my face like a hot river. A couple of hours later, I returned home only to find my mother passed out on the floor.

Fuck. She was in the recovery stages of breast cancer and occasionally passed out. I knew it was my fault. I felt like a dog. She slowly came around, and I helped her up. Neither of us spoke. We never spoke of that day again.

That was the day I knew I couldn't stay. This place would destroy me. It made me feel like I couldn't go on with life. It was a dark realisation. But I also knew what I wanted from life, what I deserved from life, and it wasn't here. So, it was all or nothing.

The next time I spoke with Bay, I brought up the topic of marriage. When we were at the airport in Frankfurt, before returning home, we had agreed that if things didn't work out, we would just get married. But she couldn't do that. She couldn't go against her parents. And as crushing as that was, I didn't want to be the reason her relationship with her family broke—or even cracked in the slightest.

I felt nothing. Empty. Alone. Her mom even called me afterward and explicitly told me to leave Bay alone. It was not an easy conversation, especially with my parents standing in the same room. My thoughts instantly turned to one thing: my dad's gun closet.

So, on Sunday, while they went to church, I took out his rifle. I had no idea how to load it, but I hoped it was already loaded. I sat on the couch with the cold metal pressed between my legs, feeling defeated. I'd been here before. I knew the process, and what it took to jump off this cliff.

For whatever reason, the phone rang—it was Bay. She had discovered the conversation that had taken place between her mother and me and wanted to call. We exchanged very few words, but she could sense the darkness consuming me. She wanted to help; she wanted to fix it. She's always been a fixer.

"What if I call Brad and see if he will marry you? It's worth a try," she said.

I just felt numb, dead inside, but she convinced me to hang on. And so, I did.

A few days later, she called me again. "He agreed. He said yes."

I didn't know what to say. I felt so drained, but I had hope. I wasn't sure what awaited me around the corner, but this felt like a lifeline. I had nothing to lose. So, I started looking into everything I would need and began planning. I didn't tell my parents anything until I had all the facts, all the details, and my paperwork in order for my flight. Once everything was set, I told them I was leaving in three days. I didn't care what they thought of me. I didn't care that I had most likely disappointed them. I didn't care that I was about to embark on something illegal. It felt like my life depended on this moment, whatever the consequences.

The packing was a haze. Everything felt like a blur. But I was detached, running on empty. On the outside, I appeared level-headed, normal—but fuck, I was broken, shredded to pieces on the inside, bleeding and unable to breathe. These few months felt like hell, like I had been captured, locked up, and beaten. There were no tears at the airport. I felt nothing.

But when I stepped through the gates and gave one final wave goodbye, and when I was finally on my own, the tears streamed down my face—tears of endurance, tears of brokenness.

Dear Mistress

A new year marks a new beginning. It's a frosty Friday morning, and I relish the quiet roads as I make my way through the countryside. There's a unique peace that comes with being alone with my thoughts, lost in my head. I enjoy my own company—perhaps more than most—but it's always been a defining part of who I am.

Seeing my Mistress has become a routine part of my life. Yet, when I think of her, I don't view her as just a Mistress. I know she prefers to maintain that boundary for professional reasons, and I fully respect that. Still, she is someone with whom I feel I can freely express the hidden corners of my mind. She embodies the kind of energy I naturally connect with in the world beyond this one.

Over the years, I've become particular about the people I surround myself with—those who genuinely have my best interests at heart. She falls into that category. I often wonder how long our journey together will last. In the short time I've known her, our sessions have brought me inner peace and calm. Many burdens from my past no longer carry the weight they once did, and that feels incredible.

As I pull into her driveway, I feel unusually distracted. We've had a longer break than usual between today's session and the last, and I can't help but feel a little tense. During previous sessions, I felt composed and focused, able to endure even the most intense moments. But today, I sense I've lost a bit of that mental equilibrium. Still, I'm here, and this familiar setting offers some comfort.

As always, the door opens before I can knock, and she welcomes me inside. She ascends the stairs with a speed I can never quite match, which makes me smile—how anyone can move with such grace in heels is beyond me.

We sit down for a brief conversation, catching glimpses of each other's lives. I was certain I wanted to pick up where we left off—with a judicial session—but deep down, I know I need something softer today. This space doesn't demand that I prove myself to anyone, which I deeply appreciate. Yet, a part of me, the self-critical part, can't help but view this as a weakness.

So, when she asks her usual question, "What are you looking for in today's session?" I reluctantly reply, "A bit of both."

She pats her lap, signalling for me to lie down, insisting I place all my weight on her. It's oddly intimidating to lie in such a vulnerable position, unable to see her but fully visible to her gaze. She begins her rhythmic hand slaps, but I already feel distracted. My mind refuses to clear. Perhaps I've had too much time to unwind after a hectic year. A week ago—right after a conversation with my mom—I would have been hyper-focused, dissecting every word of that discussion in a judicial session. Those talks always find a way to linger.

My body betrays me with shivers and shakes. *Get a grip*, I think to myself. I extend my arm for her to hold, hoping for steadiness. Sometimes, lying on her lap feels too exposing, as though she can read me completely. Every sensation feels amplified; every slap with something other than her hand stings. I grip her hand tightly, my clammy palm pressing into hers.

Then it stops. I feel raw and unprepared for the next phase: the bench, the canes. She starts gently, and I appreciate her ability to gauge the session, applying just the right amount of force. I had handcrafted a ruler for our sessions, but at the moment, I slightly regret it—it stings more than I anticipated. Still, I can't help but laugh at the irony.

She alternates between the ruler, paddle, tawse, and canes—a variety I particularly appreciate today. Occasionally, she catches me off guard, and I inhale sharply. The session concludes with six steady strokes and six quick ones. Finally, my body relaxes. She gently rubs my back as I let the rush of endorphins wash over me. For the first time, I struggle to describe how I feel. Dizzy. Tingly. Disoriented. She senses it, too.

"You weren't your usual self," she says.

"I know," I reply.

"And that's okay. It's perfectly normal," she reassures me.

We hug. I dress. I leave.

Into the Darkness

My plane landed at Heathrow early in the morning. The dull sky was grey and overcast, typical for that time of year. Bay was planning to meet me at the terminal. We hadn't seen each other in almost six months. The excitement I felt was mixed with a heaviness that weighed on me—I was emotionally drained, and the past few months had taken their toll. I felt lost. Of course, I was thrilled to see her, but I also felt like I had been through so much. I had lost myself. I was quiet, withdrawn, and unsure of who I even was anymore.

When our eyes met, we just stood there for a moment, holding each other, as though we were afraid to let go. She was visibly shocked by how I looked—tired, very skinny, and simply not myself. I could see it in her eyes, but there were no words to explain what I had been through.

We slowly made our way to Staines, where Brad was waiting to meet us. He generously offered his apartment for us to stay in for a few days while Bay was here. His kindness was overwhelming, especially considering his commitments. Those few days were a blur. I was utterly exhausted, and all I wanted to do was sleep for days. My visa meant I couldn't work for the first six months, which seemed easier when reading the stipulations than actually living through it, especially since I had arrived here completely broke. But I had no choice but to figure out a way to survive.

It was then that we came across an advert for an au pair position, offering accommodation and £80 a week cash in hand. It seemed like the perfect solution. I grabbed the opportunity, mostly for the accommodation. It was my chance to get back on my feet and also finalise the marriage. We needed two witnesses for the ceremony—something that seemed simple enough, but was made incredibly difficult because we were keeping it a massive secret. I had Bay, and Brad had to reluctantly ask one of his brothers.

The interview before the ceremony was uncomfortable. Trying to answer questions about each other felt awkward when we didn't know much beyond surface-level details. It must have seemed so obvious that this whole thing was a fake. We stumbled through so many questions, incorrectly answering or simply fumbling our way through them. But we finally completed the ceremony, and I breathed a massive sigh of relief, relieved that it was finally over—or at least, the first part of this journey.

My time as an au pair with the Turkish family was short-lived. One evening, without warning, they decided to kick me out to make room for her sister. I was given no alternatives and no explanation. It felt as if she knew the truth—that my marriage was a lie.

She and her sister exchanged glances and laughed, saying in Turkish, "You could always stay with your husband," while giving me sideways looks. Her husband, a timid and somewhat shy man, seemed embarrassed, and he felt obligated to take me somewhere.

I asked him to drive me to Brad, who was running a pub at the time. I had no other choice but to stay with him for the night. It wasn't the smoothest start, and I felt like a criminal—a foreigner, homeless, jobless, and completely broke. The lowest of society. They didn't want to pay me, and I wasn't going to beg for it.

Brad was always calm—something I appreciated amid the chaos. I hated drama, chaos, and above all, loathed feeling in debt. I had to simply endure this journey, whatever direction it took; after all, this was my choice. But it wasn't easy for someone like me, who craves control.

The next day, Brad called his mother and told her a friend needed to stay in his old room for as long as necessary. No questions asked. And she didn't ask any. She immediately drove to Staines to pick me up and took me to Reading to stay with her. I couldn't help but think how amazing it must be to have parents who genuinely respect you when you reach out, without probing. I felt so incredibly grateful to both of them.

The journey to Reading was quiet. I was acutely aware of the lies I had willingly invited into my life. That in itself was one thing, but involving others who had no idea—particularly Brad's mother—weighed heavily on my conscience. I didn't know how to be or who to be.

So, I stayed withdrawn, only speaking when spoken to, feeling like an outsider in my own life.

Their house was a typical townhouse in a row of similar homes, neat and functional. She prepared Brad's old room with fresh bedding and allowed me to settle in while she made dinner. It felt like a luxury to have a place to stay, a bed, warmth, and safety. His mom was kind in a way that felt genuine. Over the years, I've noticed that I've always connected well with older people. I often come across as quiet and hard to read, but once I open up a little, I tend to draw people in. We spent a lot of time together, and I could sense she enjoyed having me around. But it made things harder. I struggled with the internal conflict, the deceit, and the weight of it all.

Days stretch out when you have nothing to do and no sense of purpose. I had to find a way to earn money. Desperation led me to a decision I never thought I would make. With Bay's consent, we doctored her sister's passport with my photo—an act of survival, but one that filled me with guilt—and I applied for a small retail job. They didn't question much, assuming I was "European". And just like that, I got the job. It felt good to have somewhere to be, to interact with people, and to gain some independence. I earned enough to rent a room. I will forever be thankful to Brad's mom for taking me in and showing me such kindness. It was bittersweet to move out, but my conscience couldn't handle it any longer. It felt right to leave.

The retail job, in many ways, became a time for me to recharge and feel human again. The steady rhythm of folding clothes and stocking shelves gave me space to breathe, even if it was only temporary. However, it was never something I felt proud of. I kept my life a secret, avoiding anything deeper than superficial relationships with those I met. Small talk about the weather and the latest sale was easier than explaining who I was. It was safer that way—avoiding the need to lie to people. Once you start a lie, it spirals out of control like a wild bushfire you can't contain.

I met nice people, of course, but it was my conscience I battled daily, a quiet but persistent voice in the back of my mind. Deep down, I tried to remind myself that I was a good person, but my self-destructive nature was always there, a shadow lurking, reminding me of the exact opposite. The less I revealed, the safer I felt. You could never be truly sure who might turn on you or what might be used against you. This was the new me—a lone, dark soul with walls higher than the Empire State Building, carefully constructed to keep everyone at a distance.

I asked if Bay could join me over the summer, and my manager agreed. When Bay finally arrived, it helped alleviate some of the loneliness I had been feeling. Life always felt ten times better with her by my side. The summer came and went in the blink of an eye, and to be honest, those days felt like a blur. We did things—going out, hanging out with friends—but it was as if my mind couldn't grasp the daily moments. I could only recall flashbacks of the major events that took place.

Police officers made me nervous; I felt as though the word "GUILTY" was stamped on my forehead every time I passed one. I had frequent nightmares of doors being kicked in, and the terrifying thought of being arrested and deported back to South Africa haunted me. It was as though I was moving through the darkest of nights, walking on a path made of fragile eggshells, knowing that if I stepped too hard, it would all crack.

One morning, as my manager and I took the elevator down to the cafeteria at the retail shop where I worked, she looked at me with a serious expression. She wanted to offer me a promotion. I froze, completely caught off guard, and could do nothing but stare at her in silence. Her gaze seemed to pierce right through me, and I could tell she had noticed something wasn't quite right. She could read me, seeing the hidden anxiety in my eyes. My heart began to race, and I felt a cold sweat forming on my skin.

"Let's go into the office," she said, her eyes studying me intently, as though she could sense I was hiding something.

"Sit down and tell me—there's something you're not telling me," she commanded, her voice calm but with a gentle authority.

My mind was racing, but as I sat so close to her, her piercing green eyes burning into me, I couldn't bring myself to lie. It felt like an eternity before I finally spoke.

"I'm not who I said I was."

The words came out slowly, as if they were the last remnants of a defeated battle. I held her gaze, staring into her eyes, trying to read her face like a map, searching for any flicker of emotion. My mouth felt dry, but somehow, I found the strength to continue.

I began to explain my situation, speaking in broad strokes but enough to reveal the ugly truth beneath the lies. "I'm sorry for everything," I added, feeling the weight of the apology crush me.

It felt as though the world around us had paused, the silence so heavy it was almost suffocating. You could have heard a pin drop.

"Thank you for telling me. That couldn't have been easy," she said, her voice gentle yet understanding. "I get it, and if you're worried about me reporting you, don't."

I looked at her, stunned, a mix of shock, relief, and confusion washing over me. I didn't know what to say at that moment. Silent tears slipped down my face as I fought to stay composed. It was as if someone had given me a second chance at life. It felt like she saw the real me, not the person I had to be on this journey, and in that instant, I felt an overwhelming sense of gratitude.

"I will have to let you go, though—you know that," she continued, her tone soft. "But I'll give you a reference under your real name." And just like that, she stood up and embraced me.

As I turned to leave, she called out, "Do you know why I hired you?"

I paused, looking at her, slightly confused. "No," I answered quietly.

"Your handshake was firm, and you looked me dead in the eyes. I knew there was something about you," she explained.

I blushed, recalling that day—but with a slightly different version of it than hers. I remembered feeling like complete shit, locking eyes with her, fully aware of the illegality of the situation.

I gave her a slight nod, grateful for her kindness, and turned to leave. By then, the adrenaline had faded, leaving me feeling drained as I made my way home.

It wasn't the last time I saw her. We formed a friendship, meeting up frequently before she eventually returned to Sweden. It turned out our pasts had some striking similarities.

Six months had passed, and I could finally work legally under my name. The past few years had felt like a constant state of instability, but I longed for normality and stability. It was time for me to start thinking about a career path. I was clueless, with no solid experience to draw on, but I knew it was time to make a decision. I considered a few options—either a role as a legal secretary, or something in IT. I applied to a few jobs, tailoring my CV for each, depending on which path I was pursuing.

It felt like forever before I was finally called for my first interview. It was for an IT helpdesk analyst role: two weeks on, two weeks off, with rotating day and night shifts. They were looking to fill two positions, and there were two applicants—me being one of them. I fabricated some experience, just enough to make it seem remotely plausible that I could do the job. I knew I was a quick learner, and all I needed was a chance to prove myself.

Looking back at that interview, I realise how my inexperience and youthful answers must have come across as endearing, to put it politely. Despite my desperation for the opportunity, I dared to ask, outright, what my chances were of landing the role. And when I was offered the position, I boldly negotiated my salary on the spot.

I was ecstatic. Finally, something positive was happening. I had no clue about computers or anything IT-related, but the woman who interviewed me didn't seem concerned about my lack of knowledge, so I didn't dwell on it for too long. I enjoyed this role. Learning something new every day and becoming confident in delivering what was expected of me felt incredibly rewarding. Not long after I started, they switched to only day shifts, which meant that for the first time I had weekends entirely to myself. Life felt good.

I had been working in this role for almost two years when Bay and I made a routine of visiting each other as often as we could—either she would come to see me, or I'd travel to Germany to visit her. Long-distance relationships were never easy, but we managed to make it work. Time apart felt like small gaps in a much larger process, and the end goal was always to be together.

At some point, Bay decided she no longer wanted to finish her degree. Studying business had never really been her passion, and she admitted it was never something she truly desired. Her real passion was nutrition. So, she moved in with me, where I was renting a room in a shared house. She quickly found a job as a PA, and life occasionally showed glimpses of normality, but it seemed nothing was ever simple.

One of the housemates was a bit of a loose cannon, frequently spiralling out of control, which often resulted in the police showing up at all hours of the night. It wasn't the kind of attention I needed, especially considering my delicate situation. So, we decided it was time to find a place of our own, somewhere we didn't have to share with anyone else. To be honest, having our own space was a relief. I had always been someone who loved solitude and valued my privacy, except for Bay. The idea of not having to constantly deal with random people was a welcome change.

Then one day, Brad reached out to me and told me he had met someone else and that they were planning to get married. He had to tell her about us, and it caused quite a bit of tension between them. The arguments escalated so much that he felt he had no choice but to file for a divorce. I still needed two more years to get my citizenship, and suddenly everything felt like it was falling apart. It was as though the ground had been ripped out from under me. All that effort, all that time would be for nothing. I felt frozen, staring directly into the uncertainty of my future.

To make matters worse, she developed a deep hatred for me, threatening to expose everything and resorting to all sorts of intimidation. She became a ticking time bomb, ready to explode at any moment.

We had numerous exchanges trying to find some kind of solution, but it was hopeless. His mind was made up, and she wasn't budging. It was an intense, emotionally charged time, to say the least. But I wasn't going to tolerate the threats.

"Then let her go to the police," I told Brad in one of our final conversations, my internal storm suddenly as calm as the ocean after a tornado. "Because, as understanding as I am, if I go down, you'll need to explain your part in this, too."

There was a long pause before I continued, "We'll get a divorce, which I'll pay for, but I'll state the reasons, and you'll sign it. You won't bear a single cost in this."

Ever since Brad broke the news, I had been trapped in a whirlwind of emotions. The shock of it all had shaken me to my core, and I couldn't seem to find my footing. Every thought felt like a battle against my mind, as I tried to process what had just happened. I was paralysed by fear, frustration, and helplessness—too overwhelmed to eat, sleep, or even think clearly. The weight of the situation was all-consuming, and it felt like there was no way out.

I spent countless hours ruminating, my mind constantly racing, searching for a way to fix everything. But the more I thought, the more hopeless it seemed. It was like I was in a constant fog, unable to see the path forward. My body ached from the constant stress, and I felt utterly drained as if I had nothing left to give.

One day, though, something unexpected happened. My CEO—someone I had always respected for her wisdom and experience—called me into her office. She wasn't the typical corporate leader. She had a way of seeing people, understanding their struggles, and offering a sense of calm when everything seemed chaotic. She sensed that something was wrong and, without prying too much, asked what was going on. For some reason, I felt I could trust her. Maybe it was her own life experience, having recently gone through a divorce herself, or perhaps it was the way she looked at the world with an open mind. I decided to open up to her.

As I spoke, I could feel the weight starting to lift, if only a little. She listened without judgment, offering a sense of understanding that was exactly what I needed at that moment. She didn't offer empty reassurances; instead, she gave me practical advice and put me in touch with the right resources.

Within days, she connected me with a team of lawyers who specialised in situations like mine. They didn't waste time—every meeting and consultation was a step closer to resolving the mess I had found myself in. The process wasn't easy, but with the right guidance, things began to fall into place. I started to see a light at the end of the tunnel. The legalities that had seemed so overwhelming at first were now manageable, and I was finally able to take the necessary steps toward securing my future.

In the following months, I went through the divorce process with a sense of clarity I hadn't had before. I took the advice she had shared with me—patience, persistence, and the importance of seeking the right support—and applied them to every step.

And then, something incredible happened: I managed to secure my citizenship. A process that seemed like an impossible hurdle was now completed, all thanks to the support I had received at the right time. The relief I felt was immense, but it was also a bittersweet victory. The emotional toll had been heavy, but now I could look ahead with a sense of stability, knowing I had navigated one of the hardest chapters of my life.

I had learned never to take anything for granted—not the significance of what it took to earn that piece of paper. The cost wasn't financial, though. It was something much deeper. The price had been emotional—a cost that no amount of money could cover. What I had gained was freedom—something I hadn't truly known in so many years. It was like I was waking up from a long, oppressive sleep. I was finally free to be me again. But even as I tried to reclaim that sense of self, I wasn't sure what it even looked like. Who was I, after all this time? The me that had once been was buried so far under layers of survival instincts and pain that I had to dig through everything just to find a glimpse.

And yet, this newfound freedom also carried with it the weight of possibility. I could build something new. I had a chance to create a future, to shape something better after all the chaos and turmoil that had consumed me. This, I realised, had always been the goal I'd been working toward: a chance at something more than survival, something beyond the pain.

But it didn't come easy. I spent weeks—maybe even months—trying to recondition myself. I had to remind myself daily that it was me now, that the past no longer defined me. I no longer had to bow to it or carry its burdens. I was no longer trapped in someone else's narrative. The decisions were mine now. I owned my name, my life. The freedom was real. No-one could take that from me, not anymore.

Yet, even in that moment of relief, the overwhelming sense of gratitude I felt was laced with a sharp awareness of how much I still had to make up for. There was so much to give back, to atone for—wrongdoings I'd endured, and maybe even some I had caused. I wasn't sure how to reconcile the two sides of myself: the person I was becoming, and the person I had been. I wasn't even sure who that person was anymore. The fog of survival had clouded my vision for so long, and now, even as the mist lifted, I still felt a bit lost.

I didn't know how to re-enter the world. I didn't know how to fit into a society that had moved on without me. As much as I longed to contribute, to add value, I didn't know where to begin. All I wanted was to forget the past—the years spent becoming someone I had to be, just to survive. The person I had been at that time felt so distant now, yet I couldn't shake the remnants of her. It wasn't just the past that I wanted to shed, it was the way it had shaped me.

But that's when I fell into old patterns. The next few years were a blur—a chaotic mix of hard work during the week and wild nights on the weekends. I lived for the escape, indulging in alcohol and drugs. For a while, the high felt like the only thing that kept me afloat, the only way I could silence the noise in my mind. It was a fleeting freedom, though. A temporary fix. Deep down, I knew it wasn't the answer. But for a moment, it was enough to give me the illusion of relief from everything I had been running from.

In that haze, I didn't have to confront who I was, or the person I wanted to become. I just needed to feel, even if only for a few hours, that I wasn't shackled by the past anymore.

Bay and I had always dreamed of buying a house. It was one of those life goals I'd always thought about, something I was determined to achieve before turning thirty. We weren't making a lot of money, but it was the tail end of the time when a small 5% deposit was still enough to secure a place. So, we poured everything we had into it—every ounce of energy, every penny we could spare.

The moment we got the keys to our first property, it felt surreal. It felt like we had taken a huge step forward, though the weight of the mortgage payments left me with a pit in my stomach. There wasn't much room for error; every month, we had to make it work. But deep down, I knew it was the right decision. I wasn't paying into someone else's pocket anymore—I was investing in something that was ours.

Then, just as life seemed to be stabilising, I got hit with the unexpected. I was made redundant. It came completely out of the blue, and the feeling of being pushed aside was something I never wanted to repeat. There was no real explanation, just a decision made for me, one that felt like a weight crashing down, beyond my control. I remember the sinking feeling in my chest as I walked out of that office. But there was a small silver lining: a payout that allowed us to take care of something that had bugged me for months—the hideous, dirty pink bathroom suite in the house. We ripped it out and replaced it with something more fitting. A small victory in an otherwise frustrating time.

Finding a new job wasn't easy, but it was a necessary step forward. By the time I started applying, I had a bit more experience under my belt than when I had first started my career. Still, there was a hard truth I had to face: it often came down to likeability. I had my eyes on a role that I thought was perfect for me, but I didn't get it. I was disappointed, of course, but I didn't have time to wallow. I kept pushing forward, knowing that each rejection was just one step closer to where I was supposed to be.

Then, there was that one interview—a moment where I could feel something wasn't right. I just couldn't keep pretending. I remember stopping mid-conversation and simply telling them, "This isn't going to work for me." I knew right away it wasn't a good fit. Maybe some people would think that was arrogant, but after swallowing so much for so many years, I had learned to trust my instincts. I knew what felt right, and I wasn't willing to force myself into a situation that didn't align with who I was becoming.

The role I'd wanted so badly? It became available again. So, I applied once more, this time with more confidence and clarity. And this time, I got it. I was relieved—excited, even. Or so I thought.

On my first day, the excitement quickly faded. There was something about the manager that set my nerves on edge.

He strutted in, barking orders like he owned the place, tossing his jacket around like it didn't matter to him. Instantly, I knew—this wasn't for me. It was the energy I felt. I've always trusted my gut, even when it doesn't make sense to others. But it has always guided me well.

At lunch, I called Bay and simply said, "I'm not feeling it." Earlier that day, I had taken a phone interview with another company, and everything about that conversation felt right. I thought about it for a moment—should I just leave or give them a chance to explain? I wasn't one to burn bridges, but I had to stay true to myself. So, I decided to be upfront with them.

I went to the manager and, when he said, "Can I ask why?" I knew I could be brutally honest and say, "The manager's a total dick," but I chose to keep it professional. Instead, I simply said, "It's just a feeling. Sometimes, you know when something isn't right for you. And I have another offer I'd like to explore."

He looked confused. "So, you want to leave a paid role for a possible role?"

I knew it didn't make sense to him, but I stood by my decision. I said, "Yes." I shook his hand, walked out, and left that door open in case I changed my mind. They even offered me a 5K raise if I returned. But honestly? It felt good to walk away on my terms.

Fortunately, the other role panned out. The one I'd felt a connection with during the interview. It opened doors for me that I hadn't even imagined. And looking back, I realised that decision was one of the clearest and most empowering choices I'd made. I never looked back.

Focus

I find myself in a restless stage, where everything feels like a mix of contradictions, each thought fighting for clarity. I'm lost in my mind, trying to make sense of things that don't seem to fit together. It's in these moments when I'm best left alone, tucked away in the quiet of my thoughts, piecing everything together like a puzzle that refuses to align. I crave solitude; I need it, almost like a breath of air—an escape from everything and everyone around me.

I love deeply, more than most people can understand, and when I do, it's all-encompassing. I can lift someone who's at their lowest and help them see the beauty and the light they can't find in themselves at the moment. I give my loyalty fiercely, but only to a select few whom I trust implicitly, knowing they can rely on me no matter what. For me, loyalty, honesty, and zero-nonsense are non-negotiable—it's all I expect from people.

And yet, there's this paradox within me. I am incapable of receiving their kindness, their support, and their words of comfort. It's like I'm immune to accepting anything good in my life, no matter how much I long for it. I don't know why it's this way; it's just how it has always been. So, I retreat inwardly, into the safe space of my mind, where I wrestle with my thoughts until I conclude that either it makes sense, or I accept that it never will. And then, life moves on, as it always does. People disappoint me more often than not, and I find myself frustrated and annoyed at my tendency to give too much, to reveal too much of myself. It's like I'm constantly pouring myself into others and being left empty in return.

I wonder: are people so busy they can't drop everything at a moment's notice? If someone I cared about needed me, I wouldn't hesitate, no matter the distance or the circumstances. I would be there without a second thought. Does that make me naive? Foolish? Or simply hopelessly idealistic in a world that doesn't seem to care? People say the right words, they promise the world, but when it comes to living up to those words, the gap between what they say and what they do is staggering. I don't speak just to fill the silence. I say what I mean, and I feel it deeply, each word carrying weight and purpose. But in the end, I wonder if anyone else feels the same way—or if I'm just too much for this world to understand.

Either way, today I feel the weight of my mind pressing down on me. It's a feeling of exhaustion mixed with the urge to regain control and refocus my energy, my thoughts, and myself. I know that there's only one place and one person who can help me with this. I can't help but wonder—how did I even manage before? It certainly wasn't always easy to get by, but now it feels as though I'm trying to make up for all the time I lost in the past, searching for clarity.

Over time, I've noticed how much more relaxed I've become during these sessions. There's a sense of peace that comes over me. I've learned to trust her fully now.

Her energy, her approach, all puts me at ease despite it taking me a while to get here.

Today, I crave something tough, something that will help me regain control. I need to sharpen my focus, to sift through the chaos in my mind. After sharing a bit of my internal struggle with her, we begin to prepare. I slowly remove my trousers, feeling the cool air on my skin, and take a small sip of water to steady myself. She methodically arranges the bench, and I can see the canes laid out before her, each one ready for her selection. The sight of them sends a slight wave of anxiety through me, but I push it down. I know this is what I need. I'm a little nervous, remembering the last session—how I'd struggled to focus, how the pain felt overwhelming, even during the OTK. But today, I'm ready. I'm determined to block out the million thoughts swirling in my head and be fully present, to be in this moment.

The first strike lands with a sharp crack, burning against my skin like a searing reminder of what's to come. It's a sudden, intense sting that cuts through the haze in my mind. Everything goes quiet. The only sound I hear is the familiar hum of the radiator, its steady rhythm grounding me in the present. As the next few blows land, my senses sharpen. I focus on the sensation, on her precision, feeling the weight of each cane strike. My breath catches, and my mind races and slows in tandem. For a split second, I wonder if I can cope with what's coming next. But as the blows continue, I centre myself. I start to connect with the reasons I'm here, feeling each strike deep within, assigning it to the pain I carry, the ache I've tried to suppress.

I hear her breath—steady, controlled. I can feel her movements, quiet and deliberate, as she selects each cane, the soft sound of it swishing through the air before it strikes. Occasionally, the chirping of birds outside breaks the silence, a small reminder of the world beyond this room. But I push myself to stay focused, to stay in my space, lowering my head as I try to block out everything around me.

I concentrate on controlling my breathing—steady, slow. It usually takes a few strikes to get into my groove, but once I do, I can remain calm, steady, and silent. It's a strange, almost meditative state. I feel the chaos inside me begin to fade as the pain sharpens my focus. This is the moment I cherish—the moment when I finally regain control over my internal storm.

Occasionally, she shifts her technique, hitting a spot I hadn't anticipated, and it throws me off my rhythm, making my body tense. I feel the shiver of reaction crawl up my spine. Damn, I hate that feeling—when my body lets me down, betraying the calm I've worked so hard to achieve. But I push past it, focusing on the next breath, on the next strike.

The session continues, and time seems to blur. The pain, the focus, the rhythm—they all blend together, becoming part of the same experience. Soon enough, the session comes to an end. It always passes quickly when I'm this focused. When she announces the final six strikes, I feel drained and spent. But I also feel a strange sense of release—a relief that it's almost over, ready to relax, to let the emotions and endorphins flood through me.

The last blow lands, and I finally let go. Tears well up, flowing freely down my face. I don't care if she sees me crying. It's not about the pain anymore—it's about the freedom, the release, the peace that fills me as I surrender to the moment. I don't try to hide it. I let it all spill out, every tear carrying with it the tension that's been building for so long.

She attends to me briefly, tending to my backside, and then retrieves tissues. She always rubs my back gently, a comforting touch, as I slowly gather myself, preparing to stand. There's a dizzying sensation that follows, an overwhelming light-headedness that makes me grateful for the time to compose myself. I've learned not to rush. I take my time, knowing the dizziness will pass.

When I finally rise to my feet, everything feels like a haze—fuzzy, distant. But I know she's there, standing close, ready to wrap me in an embrace. And I welcome it, wrapping my arms around her, holding her tightly. It's a moment of connection, of gratitude. I probably squeeze her a little too tightly, but at that moment, I can't help myself. I'm overwhelmed with a sense of thankfulness—grateful for the space she's given me, for the release, for the way she allows me to be vulnerable, to be myself.

It's hard to explain this feeling, this bond we share. She's not the mother figure I longed for, the one I never had. But in some way, she's filled a space in my heart that I can't fully articulate. She understands me in a way that others don't, without judgment. She lets me be me— even the parts that are dark, strange, and difficult to understand. She doesn't shy away from it. She sees me, truly sees me, and accepts me without question.

To me, she's a precious gift—someone I don't take for granted, someone who has become a part of my journey in ways I can't fully express, but who I hold close to my heart all the same.

Anger

I often travelled home while I was abroad, in between the moments on my journey to freedom, trying to return at least once a year—mostly out of a sense of obligation, if I'm being honest. It always felt like a dark cloud looming over me.

I never shared my struggles with my parents. As far as they were concerned, I was thriving—constantly hopping from one place to another, living an adventurous life. They had no idea about my living conditions, and how I could barely afford a flight home each year. It wasn't that I was embarrassed or too proud—I simply kept my life separate from theirs. I didn't want them to find any enjoyment in my struggles, nor did I want them to see me as weak.

My mom used to say I wouldn't amount to anything. She often told me that I'd probably have a string of children before I ever left the house. Looking back, I wonder what those words truly meant. What did she truly feel about me? What did she think of me as a person? I relied on myself for as long as I can remember—my achievements were always mine alone. I didn't care for her approval. I didn't need her words of congratulations, because I didn't trust them. Even when she did offer them on rare occasions, they carried no warmth, no meaning.

Sometimes, Bay would come with me when I visited. It was better than going alone. Bay was the only person who had truly seen my mom for who she was—the one who never held back when it came to how she spoke to me or treated me, especially when Bay was around. I know it was hard for Bay to witness the weaker version of me that I so desperately loathed whenever I was in my mom's presence. I never spoke back. I just took it, like a dog. That's how it's always been.

The only comfort I took in it was knowing that for once, I had a witness. I wasn't crazy when I explained the things my mom did. She was the person who should have loved me the most, unconditionally, yet she made me feel like I was nothing.

I always feared that no-one would believe me. My mom is one of those people who is active in the community— always helpful, and always likeable. So, whatever she said about me, people believed. They believed I was the troubled child, the one who caused endless issues. My mom was a master manipulator, able to convince everyone that I was the problem. She felt like a force I could never beat.

For me, it wasn't about a game of who was better or who was winning—it was about wanting a normal, warm, loving relationship. But to her, it always seemed like she needed to have the upper hand. So, when I think of her, it's hard to remember any good times, because they were few and far between. When I think of her, I hear her words, I see her face—the anger, the spite, the way she would throw whatever little I shared back in my face. It's like she couldn't stop herself. I was her emotional punching bag. And sometimes, it seemed like she even took pleasure in treating me this way. It was only when I opened up to Bay about my past that she confirmed it wasn't normal.

Sometimes, when I arrived home for my two-week visit, there wouldn't even be a "Hello". Like the time my dad was ill. The first words out of my mom's mouth were, "You're late." After not seeing me for over a year, that was her greeting. "I'm going to see your dad—come if you want, or don't bother."

I wasn't shocked, though Bay stood there, completely taken aback. As much as it helped having Bay there with me, I often thought it might be better not to drag her through this. This was my family and my shit, not hers.

Whenever Bay and I both came home, we were told not to show any affection for each other, to pretend we were nothing more than friends, for the sake of the family. I despised that request. I was branded as gay, a lesbian, without ever being asked about my life. I didn't grow up gay or "in the closet". I have no issue with being gay, but I never felt the need for a coming-out conversation because, simply put, I am not gay. But it seemed easier to let them stick that label on me than to explain myself, especially since they didn't care either way. Their words of disgust were enough.

My dad, for example, refused to drink out of the same cup as me. The person I chose to be with, the one I felt drawn to, just happened to be a woman. When I look at myself, I struggle to articulate what I see. I don't always view myself as particularly feminine, or masculine. I see someone who is complex, layered—someone who doesn't fit into a box. Call it what you want, label it however it helps you understand me. But for me, that's just who and what I am. I'm drawn to the energy of a person.

What I hated most was the suffocating feeling that I had no voice, no opinions of my own. Everywhere else in my life, I never hesitated to stand up for myself or others, to speak my mind without fear, and to be brutally honest about how I felt. I was known for it. I was the one who didn't back down, and who never let anyone push me around. But with my mom, it was different. With her, I swallowed my words in silence, letting them churn inside me until they became a weight too heavy to carry. She had the power to silence me without saying a word, and I let her. Every time, I let her.

There was one occasion when I visited home, and the constant arguments became too much to bear. The tension had been building, and I reached a breaking point. Without a second thought, I decided to change my flight and leave early. Originally, I had planned to visit Bay in Germany after my stop in South Africa, but back then, I needed a visa to travel. With no money for accommodation and nowhere else to turn, I made the desperate decision to sleep on the streets of London for a week. A week that felt more like six months.

The experience was sobering, a brutal reminder of how quickly life can take a different turn. I had always told myself I was different, that I would never end up like them—people whose lives seemed like they were spiralling out of control. But deep down, I knew how easily I could find myself in the same situation. There was nothing that separated me from them. We were all just one misstep away from disaster. That realisation hit me hard, and it ignited something inside me. That was the moment I became determined to buy a house one day before I turned thirty. I needed something to hold onto, something that would prove I could change the course of my life, that I could make a choice and take control.

For me, it was essential to be independent—both financially and emotionally. The years of harsh words and painful actions had left deep scars. Their actions spoke louder than any words ever could, and they justified themselves time and again. "Your brother needs more help than you." "Your brother has a family now, kids. We want to help him with a house." Over and over, they would list all the financial support they'd poured into my brother, never once pausing to consider how I might feel.

My mom would always say, "It's your dad's money, it's his choice. I can't influence him to give you anything." Inside, I was seething. I expected her to stand up for me, to fight for me. How could she not understand that? For them, it was always about money, but for me it was about loyalty, fairness, and equality. It wasn't about needing the money—it was about knowing they had my back, that they cared enough to show up for me, the way they so clearly showed up for him.

I longed for something deeper—like a warm embrace, and unconditional love. Long phone calls, sharing the ups and downs of life, hearing about theirs in return. A connection built on genuine love and care. But instead, I was left feeling empty. I didn't care about money. It was almost insulting. What I wanted most was the kind of support that couldn't be measured in currency but in the warmth of an embrace.

Ever Thine Ever Mine
Ever Ours...

I had never believed in marriage, nor had I ever imagined myself getting married. My vision was always of being single, perhaps with one child. But then I met Bay.

Life slowly began to change in ways I hadn't expected. It became more stable, more grounded, exactly as I had always hoped. I felt more settled within myself, rediscovering who I was—a better version of myself. Surrounded by great friends, life was good. And now, I was engaged to Bay, planning our wedding. It felt like everything was falling into place.

We found a charming cottage in Devon for our ceremony—a beautiful stone house, intimate and limited to just 30 guests. It was perfect. From the flowers to the catering, we meticulously planned every detail. We opted for a small, intimate celebration with those closest to us, a testament to our journey together. One of my fondest memories was sharing all of this with Bay—the joy of building something together, from the ground up.

To announce our engagement and relationship, we sent out wedding invitations to our friends and family. I had always kept my personal life private, so it came as a surprise to many—though a pleasant one. Some had already suspected, and for them, it was just confirmation of what they'd felt. But for me, it was a moment to share our love openly, to invite others into our world, even if only for a day.

Deciding not to invite my parents was a significant moment, a conscious step toward asserting my independence. This was my life, my path, and I wanted my big day to be free from negativity, free from the expectations that had often weighed me down. It was my day, and I wanted to celebrate it on my terms.

The second stand I made was to drop my last name. It came about during one of those quiet evenings with Bay, a bottle of wine between us as we talked about our future. I didn't want to take my last name, nor did I want to take hers. A double-barrelled last name wasn't appealing to me either.

"Let's combine the letters of both our last names and see what we get," I suggested. So, after a few more glasses of wine, we started playing with the letters, tossing out combinations, until we finally landed on something that felt just right. A unique last name— our own. It was a small but powerful choice. A new legacy was born, and it felt exciting, full of potential and promise.

We didn't want the typical hen do, as I was never one for traditions. Instead, we decided to spend the evening before the wedding with all our friends who were attending. We had a lovely dinner together, spending the evening drinking, smoking cigars, and simply enjoying each other's company. It felt like a true privilege to have everyone there traveling so far to share in our special day. Their presence made everything even more meaningful, a reminder that we were surrounded by people who cared enough to be part of our journey.

The next day began with preparations: coordinating with the florist, finalising details with the caterers, setting up tables, and decorating everything with poison ivy. The tables were adorned with vibrant flowers, more ivy, and black napkins, while black bows graced the chairs. It was simple yet elegant, exactly as we had envisioned. We even decorated wheelbarrows, filled with ice, to create a "Help Yourself" bar—because we planned for enough alcohol. The spare room was set up for the ceremony, and before we knew it, time had flown by.

Everyone had warned us, "Enjoy every minute, because time will pass quickly." And they were right—time slipped away faster than we could keep up with.

As we were upstairs getting ready, our guests began to arrive. I had my best woman, Miss D, by my side, ensuring everything went smoothly. I consider her my sister—one of my truest and most loyal friends. And I had a best man, Nick. The love and support surrounding me that day were overwhelming. There are no words to fully capture the emotions I felt inside.

I remember feeling a mix of nerves and excitement. Bay's father walked her down the stairs first, while I chose to walk alone. I never imagined I would, but at that moment, I felt complete. It was a personal choice, one that felt right, and it was a moment I will never forget.

The ceremony passed in the blink of an eye; it was everything we had dreamed of and more. Afterward, we took a few photos, but then we finally allowed ourselves to relax and immerse ourselves in the celebration. The fact that all of Bay's family was there, supporting us, was truly amazing. The atmosphere was so relaxed and joyful—everything about the day felt special, unforgettable, and perfectly ours.

Pushed to the edge

Today was a short catch-up. "How are you?" It's direct, no delay tactics, but I don't mind. "What is it you're after today?" she asks, getting straight to the point.

"Today, I want to leave it up to you. I want you to push me harder than you ever have. I want to feel pain. I don't want you to be kind to me." There, I said it—straight up. With her, I can freely express my darker side.

"Okay," she replies. "We'll go to the bench then, because I know you consider OTK to be kind."

I feel a rush through my body, knowing I've just given up my control, allowing her to take the lead. And with that, a slight panic sets in. "Why are you looking at me like that?" she says, snapping me back to the moment.

Shit, I thought. She can read me perfectly, and her response is quick and spot-on.

"You should be afraid of what's coming," she says with humour, so direct and honest.

Internally, I can't help but smile at the irony of it all—her sharp wit, my request for her to push me further than she ever has—and the curious fact that, in this very moment, I feel a flicker of fear. As I slowly remove my trousers, doubt begins to seep in—will I truly be able to handle what's coming next? But even as uncertainty lingers, I force myself to maintain an air of calm and composure.

The bench is prepared as always, and I take my position. The first strike hits, and I tense up instantly. Shit, I think. She's about to deliver exactly what I asked for. I need to raise my internal bar if I'm going to get through the next 60 minutes of this. I hold my breath, anticipating the next strike. It comes quickly, and so do the ones that follow. I feel like there's no time to compose myself between blows. Shit, she's definitely pushing me. She changes sides, swaps canes, and then goes from cane to paddle.

Internally, I feel chaotic. Some blows I count as 6, others 8, even 10. I don't know what's coming next, what to expect. I'm losing control. Every now and then, she aims at my sweet spot. I feel lost inside, tempted to grab her hand just to make her pause briefly. But I can never show her weakness—it's enough that I've allowed her full control.

I hide my face deeply in my arms. It's easier not to know what's coming, to not see what she chooses, but every now and then, I catch a glimpse of her taking aim. I wiggle a bit, trying to buy myself a little time to compose myself.

"You need to hold still," her voice commands, full of authority, forcing my cooperation with just a few words.

Wow. Suddenly, I realize that all the times before she had actually been relatively easy on me. This... is a whole new level.

But I also know I can handle this. I am resilient. My mind won't crack despite all the racing thoughts. She's relentless, but I feel grateful that she is delivering exactly what I asked for without hesitation. My body shivers and shakes, betraying me—the strength of my mind doesn't match the weakness of my body.

After a while, she announces the last 6 strikes, followed by 6 quick ones to conclude.

"I think we need to stop," she says. "Your bottom has taken enough."

No, I think to myself, I can handle more. I can take it. Yet, part of me longs for peaceful release, to embrace it fully, to let go of the chaos and surrender. After all, she's the one who taught me to be kinder, more accepting of myself—the very reason I'm here. The conflict within me swirls, but I choose not to protest. After all, it feels good in a way to let go of control, to simply surrender to the moment. I feel lighter, freer, not emotional, but as if I'm in a bit of a trance. The noise in my mind fades, and I feel a surprising sense of clarity, a peace that has eluded me for so long.

I don't know why, but I feel like grabbing her hand, holding it close as I just lay there, basking in the peace. This session had been exactly what I needed—a wake-up call that realigned my perspective. It wasn't about pain or control—it was about release, about clarity.

"This was a tough session," I say as I get up, my voice raw but honest. The words feel like a confession, and I appreciate the freedom to express them. I don't hide it—I've faced something challenging, and I can admit it. This shared experience in the moment is unique, knowing that she must focus on giving just as much as I do on receiving. "You're so resilient," she says. "I don't know if that's good or bad", she continuous and I often wonder the same. I suppose it can be both.

She opens her arms, ready to embrace me. I willingly surrender to the moment, which has become a grounding act. In these moments, she reassures me and offers comfort and warmth. It is in these moments that she reminds me I am worthy of love and kindness. She has pushed me to achieve what I needed and wanted, and I leave feeling like I have perspective again.

Next Generation

Married life felt peaceful and easy with Bay. During the week, we focused on our work, and on weekends, we relished the simplicity of long walks with our dog or exploring new places together. We both loved being outdoors, immersed in nature—it was our way of recharging and grounding ourselves. As many of our friends began settling down, moving into new homes and planning families, I felt a pull to return to something I had always loved: hockey.

I had never been able to commit to a team sport before, not with the unpredictability of my past. But this time, it felt different. Joining the club gave me more than I could have imagined. It wasn't just about the sport—it was about finding a sense of belonging, something I had longed for. There were some wonderful people, especially from the "older" generation, who took me under their wing and welcomed me with open arms.

I eagerly anticipated training on Wednesdays and games on Saturdays. With each passing week, my skills improved, and by the end of a few seasons, I was leagues ahead of where I had started. But more than the skill development, it was the camaraderie that I cherished—the thrill of winning together and the sense of community that came from being part of something bigger than myself. For the first time, I truly felt like I was part of a team—not just in the game, but in life.

It was during this time that the possibility of having children one day first crossed our minds. We were inspired by another couple who had recently welcomed twins through fertility treatments. We often discussed the idea, but it always felt like an impossible dream—something that belonged to another life, one we hadn't fully embraced yet. Bay was made for motherhood and I could see that, but as for me, I liked the idea in theory. I imagined it in fleeting moments, but it never seemed to fully settle in my heart.

I was keenly aware of the freedom that came with not having kids. Our life, as it was, felt perfect. Maybe I was too selfish, too comfortable in the life we had built. The thought of children excited me briefly, but it always faded quickly. I could never picture myself sharing my space with anyone—let alone little ones running around that I'd be responsible for. But here I was, married, and everything had changed.

We had been married for about four years, and while we often talked about getting another dog, I could see a longing in Bay for something more. She always denied it, but I could see it in her eyes. I didn't want to be the reason she felt incomplete, nor did I want to hold her back from experiencing everything she wanted in life. I couldn't bear the thought of losing her. We were both well into our thirties, and time was no longer on our side.

One day, as we were walking together, I took a deep breath and said, "Let's look into having kids."

Her face lit up instantly, and I could see the joy in her eyes. It was the first time I had said those words, and seeing her reaction made me realise just how much she wanted this. I could never bear to see her unhappy. She was my constant, my most loyal companion. I would give anything for her happiness—whatever it took.

*

Needless to say, Bay wasted no time looking into clinics, figuring out what we needed, and organising everything. I tend to leave the finer details to her in certain aspects, because I know she's more than capable of handling them. This marked the beginning of a long and challenging process, one filled with many ups and downs. The first step was getting a recommendation from our GP and undergoing a few basic tests. Unfortunately, that turned out to be a disaster. The results showed that Bay's chances of conceiving were nearly impossible. She was devastated.

As for me, I tend not to get phased by obstacles easily. I've always had a tendency to want to prove the world wrong. "Don't worry about it; we'll figure it out," I reassured her.

I tried to keep her positive, adamant that this was just a small bump in the road. But even though I didn't show it, doubts were creeping in. I couldn't help but feel the weight of what we were up against.

Eventually, we found a clinic we were both happy with. They were incredible throughout the entire process, supportive and professional every step of the way. The doctor glanced at the test results and seemed completely unfazed. "Don't worry about these," he said with a reassuring smile. "We see this all the time, and we have ways around it." We exchanged a look of relief—finally, a glimmer of hope.

And that's how it all began.

Next came more tests—lots more tests. *A far cry from anything romantic*, I thought to myself. Each step felt more clinical, more impersonal, and I couldn't help but feel vulnerable, placing all our hopes in someone else's hands. But this was our journey together, and despite the uncertainty, we knew we were in it together.

I lost count of how many trips we had to make to the clinic before we could even begin the insemination process. The logistical challenges were endless, but the hardest part by far was choosing a donor. It was nerve-wracking, an overwhelming responsibility, knowing that the person we chose would have a lasting impact on our child's life. There wasn't much to go on, especially after the law had changed, allowing children to request identifying information about their donor when they turn 18.

The details we had were limited: hair colour, eye colour, occupation, height, and hobbies. Some donors listed "making things" as a hobby. Making things? Cards? Candles? Bombs? My mind definitely had its moments of doubt, spiralling into bizarre thoughts. I even had nightmares of our child looking like some strange, non-human creature. But, despite those fleeting doubts, I had to remind myself of the incredible gift this person was offering—the opportunity to help make someone else's dreams come true. After all, these children would be part me, part Bay, and that was what mattered most.

It was very important to us that we choose a single donor, for the two children we planned to have. We always agreed to each mother one child, and I always envisioned them having a special bond—one of fierce loyalty and love. We narrowed it down to two potential choices and eventually selected the one we truly felt drawn to. To our surprise, he had included a letter, sharing more about himself and his reasons for participating in the process.

Although I didn't know this person, I felt deeply moved by his words. There was such honesty, kindness, and warmth in his story that we were left speechless. It felt like a sign—an affirmation that we were exactly where we were meant to be in our lives at that moment. His words gave us the reassurance we needed, and for the first time in this process, I felt at ease, excited for the future ahead.

Before we could begin the insemination process, we had one session left: meeting with the clinical psychiatrist. It was the one session I dreaded most. Maybe it was because I always felt judged, like someone was going to dissect my inner thoughts. I had never been comfortable with the idea of speaking to a therapist. I never truly believed they could offer much. Sure, you talk, they listen, and maybe they offer some different perspectives on life. But your past and your life are what they are—unchangeable. Perhaps I just never took well to advice, as I was so used to relying on myself. Either way, I just wanted to get this over with.

We stepped into her office and greeted each other. I remained reserved while Bay was much better at the pleasantries. The conversation was relaxed, just getting to know us a little better. There were plenty of questions, some more personal than others. But the most probing one was about our emotional maturity. She turned to me, having noticed I had been quietly observing, letting Bay answer most of the questions.

"What about you?" she asked, her gaze focused on me. "How do you feel knowing you won't be biologically connected to the child?"

I paused for a moment, gathering my thoughts before I responded. The question was loaded, but I didn't want to back down.

"I know exactly how it feels to not be biologically connected to a parent," I began slowly. "To wonder about someone whose DNA I share but have never met. I know this won't be an issue for me, because I will love them unconditionally, always. And when the time comes, when they get curious and start asking questions, I will guide them and support them. I understand the guilt they may feel, even wanting to ask—wanting to know. But I know I have what it takes to hold that space for them. And I won't doubt their love for me, or question it, because I get it."

And with that, we concluded the conversation—there wasn't much more she could say about it. It's not that I mind talking about being adopted, but the perceptions around it were always something I never liked. I was acutely aware, especially within the family, that we had been adopted. If anything, it often made me feel like an outsider. My parents would frequently point out that certain facts should remain within our close circle. "Otherwise, the family will say it's because you're adopted." It carried a certain stigma, one that I never appreciated. It was as if being adopted was something to hide, something that made us different in a way that needed to be explained or excused. That burden, that subtle sense of "otherness", was something I carried with me, even when I didn't show it.

Finally, after months of tests and questions, we were ready to begin the insemination process. Bay ordered the necessary drugs to inject herself with, and it felt like an exciting, albeit nerve-wracking, new stage in our journey. Every other day, we returned to the clinic, where they would measure the growth of the follicles, ensuring there weren't too many and that they were all the right size. Ideally, we needed 2-3 good-sized follicles before the final step—insemination.

When insemination day arrived, it felt like waiting for a special occasion—endlessly drawn out, and then suddenly it was here. The sperm was washed, appearing as clear as water. I couldn't help but wonder if it was truly sperm or just water. I always felt a little mistrustful when I had no control over what was happening. But just like that, it was over. All that was left was to take it easy and wait for two weeks. The waiting felt like an eternity, each day stretching on forever. But during that time, we spent hours dreaming about our baby, imagining what they would be like. It was a hopeful, almost magical period.

Sadly, Bay didn't fall pregnant on the first try, or the second. Doubts began to creep back in, and I couldn't shake the thought of that first result from the GP. Was he right? Was this what he had meant? By the third attempt, the excitement had faded, replaced with an unsettling mix of stress and pressure. There was more to lose now. We were on our third vial, and if this didn't work, we might need to consider other options. I tried not to dwell on it, but it wasn't easy. This whole process had already taken nearly two years, and the thought of it not working out was devastating.

I could see how painful it had become for Bay now. Each injection, administered in the stomach, was taking its toll. Light bruises were starting to appear, a stark reminder of the sacrifices she was making. Finally, we were back at the clinic, ready for the insemination. The ride there was noticeably quieter than all the previous ones. There was an unspoken tension between us, something heavy that we couldn't shake. When we entered the room, there were more people than usual, and I could feel the pressure mounting. It made me uneasy.

They struggled to find her cervix, and I could feel myself becoming restless. The discomfort in the room mirrored my own. I felt like I might lose my composure at any moment. They tried, and tried again—numerous attempts, but no success. Blood was now visible, and

I could see how much pain and discomfort Bay was in. I wanted to be strong for her, but inside I was beginning to crack.

They changed tactics, brought in a different nurse, and even used the scanner on her stomach to try to locate the right spot. After what felt like an eternity, they finally found it. We could see the sperm making its way in, and for a moment, it felt surreal. I thought to myself, *It has to work. It has to.* They positioned it as carefully as they could. There were over a billion sperm in that vial—surely one of them would find its way in.

We were both exhausted, physically and emotionally. The whole experience had been so intense. Bay had always felt that the first insemination hadn't worked because she had been too active, so for this third attempt, I insisted she rest. I forbade her from lifting so much as a finger—she was to relax, watch TV, or read. I know I probably drove her crazy during those two weeks, but I couldn't help myself. Every moment felt like it mattered.

As the two-week wait neared its end, I remember driving somewhere when the news came that the sky would be filled with multiple shooting stars that night. It sounds silly, even as I say it, but in that moment I felt in my heart that it was a sign. I just knew, deep down, that this had to be it. This had to be the moment we'd been waiting for.

That Sunday, we decided to take a test a little early—just by 2-3 days, but still. We chose the digital test, the one that simply says "pregnant" or "not pregnant", because I had grown tired of second-guessing that faint blue line. It's amazing how your eyes can play tricks on you.

And then there it was: "Pregnant". We both froze. We couldn't believe it. We just stared at it, as if the words weren't quite real. I wanted to believe it, but doubts lingered. Maybe it was a false reading, since we had tested a bit early. Still, my heart raced with excitement and joy. We didn't know what to do with ourselves—it was overwhelming.

"Okay, if it's positive tomorrow, I'll believe it," I said to Bay, trying to steady myself. The next morning, with great anticipation, we tested again—and another positive result appeared. It was real. We were over the moon. The world seemed to blur around us; I couldn't focus, couldn't think straight. We were both so happy, it was as if time stood still for a moment.

We decided not to tell too many people during the first trimester, and those we did tell were sworn to secrecy. Bay didn't suffer too badly with morning sickness, so it felt like life continued as normal. But for me, everything changed. I became a bit of a nightmare, watching her like a hawk, ensuring that nothing she ate or did could possibly harm the baby. I took on everything—cleaning, shopping, you name it. I was exhausted, but I didn't mind. She was giving me a child, and I felt like I was contributing my part.

I decided to break the news to my parents, half knowing how they would respond. But I did so anyway. I was going to be a parent, and I was proud of that. Of course, my parents didn't see it the same way.

"Why do you have to bring them into sin? It's one thing that you chose this life, but now you're bringing a child into it," they said.

I didn't care about their opinion. I was happy with the life I had built for myself, and I wasn't here to convince them or beg for their acceptance. I told them because I felt obligated, though my sense of obligation had lessened over the years.

Bay's parents, on the other hand, were over the moon. Her mom loved the role of both mother and grandmother, and the thought of not having more grandchildren saddened her. They shared in our journey from beginning to end, eagerly awaiting the arrival of their grandson.

September is a somewhat busy time of year to be going into labour, with hospitals often overcrowded. Bay was in the hospital for a full seven days before our little man finally decided to arrive. I think I met the entire maternity staff during that time. Labour is nothing like how it's portrayed in the movies—it's long, tiring, and often boring for the one waiting. I now completely understand how men must feel on the other side of this experience. There were a lot of complications. Before we went in, Bay had explicitly told me she wanted a natural birth and that, if offered an epidural, I should insist they not give it to her.

After 15 hours of labour, the midwife started getting concerned about the amount of blood Bay was losing.

People were constantly coming in and out, and I could tell they were worried.

"We need to give her an epidural," one of the midwives said to me.

I was worried, exhausted, and confused, but still I insisted that it wasn't her wish. But they insisted. I remember feeling like I had let her down, but at the same time, I had to trust their judgment. Bay seemed fine, but as they prepared her for an emergency C-section, I fell apart. I felt completely drained, and I cried. I wanted to break down completely—it was just too much.

The theatre was bright and quiet, like the moon, with everyone playing their part in preparing for what was to come. It was surreal. Everything I wanted, the journey, the road that had led us here—all of it was coming to a head. I was so emotional. I made sure not to look scared; I would have surely passed out if I saw them cutting into her.

It was strangely quiet as we waited, and then, there he was—small, scruffy, and wrinkled, like a little old man. Our son. They quickly whisked him away, and I remember feeling a wave of panic. There was no cry, no sound. Was he okay? No-one said anything. They all looked so calm, even though they were frantically moving around. Then, he cried— short, quiet sobs.

They asked if I wanted to cut the cord. I couldn't fully take it all in. He was my son, and yet I didn't know him at all, but I already felt such overwhelming love and protectiveness for him. They took him over to Bay, and I could see the love in her eyes. It was the three of us, all of a sudden, and I didn't mind sharing her with him or him with her. It felt right.

One of the nurses asked if I wanted to dress him, and before I could even think, the word "No" flew out of my mouth. I was terrified I would drop him or somehow hurt him. She could probably tell I was petrified, so she insisted, gently, almost like a patient, loving grandmother. "No, you can do it."

I picked him up, and it felt as though my legs had turned to jelly. There was a ringing silence in my ears, a sensation I strangely experienced every time I picked him up in the following months. His tiny foot was the size of my thumb, and he was still curled up in the foetal position. Dressing him in the tiny outfit we had chosen for him felt like an impossible task.

I wasn't allowed to stay in the hospital, so after making sure Bay was okay and had everything she needed, I left. It was almost 6 a.m. by the time I got home. I called family and close friends to break the news and briefly share the experience, and everyone was thrilled to hear that all had gone well. They couldn't wait to meet our little man. I couldn't wait until visiting hours opened so I could see them both. All I wanted was to bring them home.

Becoming a parent is a strange feeling. Even though I was a parent now, I still didn't feel like a mature adult, let alone a responsible one. It was as though something huge had shifted, yet I was still the same person, unsure of how to carry this new responsibility.

We both decided to begin the process for my pregnancy, considering how long it had taken for Bay to fall pregnant. It felt surreal to go through it all again, especially after having just witnessed Bay's journey not so long ago. Watching her go through everything—the pregnancy, the birth—didn't exactly appeal to me. If I could fast forward, I would have. The thought of my body changing, the idea of not being able to play hockey, and the inevitable awkward moments of having to be in compromising positions with strangers—it wasn't exactly my vibe. But we had made a pact: one of each. I knew this was our path, and I would do it for our family, despite my reservations.

I equally struggled with my perception of myself. Being pregnant felt like such a distinctly female experience, and I didn't see myself in that role. I wasn't sure how to connect with or fully embrace that side of things.

I was relieved to know that we wouldn't have to go through all the consultations Bay had endured and could just jump straight into the process. But our first consultation turned out to be a shock. We had clearly misunderstood something in the fine print—perhaps about the amount of sperm available to us or the fact that we should have reserved more once we had used the three vials from Bay. Regardless of the details, there was no sperm left. It felt shattering. I didn't want another donor. I wanted our kids to share the same donor. It may sound trivial to some, but it was important to us, and I couldn't shake the feeling of loss.

The clinic was very helpful in trying to resolve our predicament. "There is a woman we know who may no longer wish to use her last vial; we could ask her if she's willing to let it go to you." My mind went blank as I tried to absorb what they were telling us. "We could also reach out to the donor to see if he would be willing to donate more, but it's quite a process, and he may not want to."

I appreciated their willingness to help, but I was still so convinced that he would say yes. After reading his letter, I was certain—*he has to say yes. He just has to.* The ride back home was a blur. I had nothing to say. I felt empty, sad, and incredibly angry at myself for missing such a crucial detail. How could I have overlooked it?

The following day, the clinic returned our call. "He said he needs time to think about it and will let us know, but the lady agreed to give you her last vial." A small sigh of relief escaped me, but along with it came the heavy weight of pressure—this would have to work the first time. At least we had one try while we waited for his decision, but the uncertainty gnawed at me. Being at the mercy of others, not having control over something so personal, was incredibly difficult.

I waited for the hockey season to finish before starting the insemination. I was nervous, yet strangely calm. I had always had a feeling I would fall pregnant easily. Still, it was different this time, already blessed with one child. Miss D was taking care of our son so we could go to the clinic without worrying about feeding or diaper changes.

I had three good-sized follicles, and while I was hopeful, I couldn't help but feel nervous about the possibility of twins. Not that I would be ungrateful, but with a three-month-old baby at home already, the idea of twins felt overwhelming.

The insemination went smoothly—over and done with in ten minutes. Secretly, I hoped this would be our last visit to the clinic. As humbling as the process was, I was reaching my limit of having our lives and bodies on display for strangers.

I don't know why, but I just knew I was pregnant. I didn't feel any physical change in my body, but there was a deep sense of certainty. So, when I took my first pregnancy test 2-3 days early and received a negative result, I couldn't believe it. I chose not to believe it. "It's because I tested early," I told myself. "I'll test again tomorrow." The following day, I could barely wait for my first morning toilet break.

Fuck. Negative again. I still refused to believe it. My intuition had never been wrong before—rarely, at least. The next day came—the official day I should have tested—and I tested negative once more. At this point, it wasn't even about not being pregnant. It was about my certainty being shattered. I couldn't accept that I had misread my own energy. Had I been arrogant, thinking I would fall pregnant on the first try? It was a hard pill to swallow, but I couldn't let go of the hope that I had gotten it right.

"Take another test tomorrow before we call the clinic to let them know it was unsuccessful," Bay's words pierced through the chaos in my head. So, the next day, I decided to take one last test, hoping for something different.

"Pregnant."

I knew it! My heart soared. We were shocked, speechless, overwhelmed by the rush of emotions. It was a feeling so surreal, almost too good to be true. After all the uncertainty, the doubts, and the waiting—here it was. The answer we had longed for.

I barely peed on the stick before the sickness hit me. I remember returning home, and the entire house smelled... different, off. Whatever it was, it wasn't a pleasant smell—it made my stomach churn. It felt like my senses were heightened, like a wild animal able to detect danger from miles away.

It started with vomiting 4-5 times a day. "It's morning sickness, it's normal," people would say. But it didn't feel normal to me. I couldn't even stand the scent of Bay's skin. The vomiting felt violent, like my insides were coming out, as though I might break a rib from the force.

I couldn't work; even light made it worse. Everything made it worse. Just walking a few steps would set me off. I was bedridden, unable to eat anything— everything came back up. It was relentless. I threw up 20-30 times a day, no exaggeration. It was exhausting. I was signed off work for three months, unable to do anything. I spent day and night in isolation, leaving Bay to care for our son while maintaining her full-time job. It was a bit of a relief knowing her mom would come to support her as long as we needed, which eased my guilt just a little.

The diagnosis was hyperemesis gravidarum—the term for this debilitating pregnancy sickness. The only thing that helped was being hooked up to an IV drip to get fluids into my body, but that meant going to the hospital, being exposed to the light, people, and all the smells that made everything worse. The other treatment was Zofran—a drug typically prescribed to cancer patients to help with nausea. However, the only way it would stay in my body was if Bay injected it into my backside.

I felt guilty for taking so much medication during my pregnancy. Every pill, every injection seemed like a reminder of how far I had fallen from what I expected my pregnancy to be. Eventually, I returned to work part-time, though by then, I was completely and utterly broken. The pregnancy had taken a toll on my body, and I had to relearn what it felt like to have an appetite again, to feel hungry. The simplest things that others take for granted had become distant memories. But through it all, despite the exhaustion and the physical strain, it was all worth it—the pain, the struggle.

On Boxing Day, we welcomed our second child into the world. Our family was complete, and I couldn't have been happier. Something inside me shifted when I gave birth. Perhaps it was all the hormones, or maybe it was the weight of the journey we had just completed, but it felt as though maternal instinct flooded me like a wild river. Giving birth, going through that experience, made me a better mother to both our boys. It brought out a whole new side of me that's hard to describe—a fierce, protective love that I hadn't fully known before.

I didn't have a maternal figure to guide or support me like most women do. There was no blueprint for how to be the kind of mother I wanted to be. I simply did what felt right, and in those moments of doubt, I always had Bay there to reassure me. Her presence was a constant, and that was enough.

But it also stirred something deep within me, opening up a pain I thought I had buried and forgotten about—something I believed was no longer an issue. It made me acutely aware of the innocence of a child, of how easy it is to love unconditionally, and that deep, innate need to protect and nurture.

I used to feel such anger towards my biological mother for abandoning me, for not fighting for me, for not choosing me. But now, I felt an incredible sadness for her. How hard must it have been to let me go? What must she have felt in the days leading up to my adoption, and in the aftermath?

And then there was my adoptive mother, a woman who couldn't have children of her own, who had been given the priceless gift of motherhood. But she also destroyed me—the pain she caused, the trauma she put me through. I felt anger towards her. Unforgivable anger.

Nine months after the birth of our second son, my father passed away. I didn't learn of his passing until after it had happened—after the funeral, after the spreading of his ashes. My mother made the decision to handle it this way, once again taking away my voice and my right to have a say. Even now, because of how everything was handled, I can't quite pinpoint the exact day he passed, only that it was in November. The fact that I experienced my father's passing in such a detached way sometimes makes me feel as though it's just a dream—that he's still alive—only for reality to hit me moments later that he truly did pass.

When the phone rang and I saw my mother's number, I knew instantly that something major had happened. I wanted to leave, to be alone. So, I did—out of sight, just by myself, crying. I don't know why, but I sent him a text message, telling him I was sorry and that I would miss him. It was my way of saying goodbye, though it felt so inadequate. I had known he was sick and in the hospital, and I'd had this nagging feeling his time was near, but I couldn't bring myself to call him. A moment I regret.

I started calling my mother less. Something about her decision made me lose respect for her. I can't explain why or pinpoint the exact moment, but it felt like the last straw—like the bond we had was shattered beyond repair. And when I lost respect for her, something shifted in how I felt about her. We became strangers.

To this day, I struggle to say the words "I love you," even though I speak them when I do call. I hate myself for it. I endure these conversations with her, but there's no warmth in them, no connection. I struggle to forgive, even though I don't hate her. It's just that forgiveness feels so distant, like something I should feel, but can't quite grasp.

I can't explain why I can't just say to her, "You broke me, you hurt me, you hated me, you chose others over me, you made me feel like my life wasn't worth living, you failed me. You did not deserve to have me." These are the truest words of how I feel, yet I feel guilty for thinking them, feeling them, and even considering saying them. Part of me feels like she must know. She could reach out to me anytime, but she doesn't. And if I don't call, then I'm the one who has forsaken her.

There's also a part of me that feels pity for her—she has no-one left except for my brother and I who live in different countries. I'm sure those words would hurt her deeply, and even now, I feel like I don't want to cause her the pain she caused me. It makes me feel pathetic. But I cannot, and will not, speak my truth because I also feel that it's a mother's duty to ensure her children are okay, loved, and cherished. It was never supposed to be my role to make sure she felt loved, understood, or like she belonged. I was the child. I'm still the child.

*

I decided to look up my family to find closure. But I was told my birth mother passed away at the young age of 18. It was a massive blow. I will never meet her, never get to know her. My gut tells me she may have committed suicide—that she couldn't overcome the emotional turmoil of giving me up. I feel it deep within me, but it's still a long journey to discover exactly what happened. Do I still have any family left? Grandparents, aunts, uncles? Would they care enough to meet me, or would I only remind them of a time in their lives they tried hard to forget?

I would have looked for her. I would have found her. The thought saddens me. All the time we could have had together still. And when I found her, I would have forgiven her. I would have wanted to understand her, to know the woman who gave me life.

It's strange how life can turn out sometimes. I've endured so much, yet everything I've gone through—the pain, the hurt—has shaped me into who I am today. I am surrounded by love, blessed to experience life, and lucky to be alive. I take nothing and no-one for granted, especially not the family I have now.

There will always be a part of me that struggles with certain elements of my past. After all, they are part of who I am. Along the way, so many people have helped change and shape the course of my life. So many, whom I will be forever grateful for. But there are two women who stand out above the rest.

The first and foremost is my beloved wife, my soulmate. She is not only the most loving friend and wife but also an extraordinary mother to our children, embodying everything I could ever have hoped for in a life partner. Throughout every challenge and triumph, she has stood steadfastly by my side. She has witnessed my darkest and most difficult moments—times when I felt unloveable, incomprehensible, and inscrutable—but her unwavering presence never faltered. Her quiet yet immense strength has been the cornerstone that holds our family together, then and now. With her, I feel complete, knowing that her love and support are constants in my life.

The second is my Mistress—a woman who played a crucial role in unlocking the hidden depths of my past. With the maturity of adulthood and a more refined perspective, the bench became a sanctuary—a place where I could release some of my deepest pain. With each strike she delivered, her precision allowed me to reset, to refocus, and to confront emotions I had buried for so long. Her lap offered me a space where I could be vulnerable, where I didn't have to hide behind walls of strength or pride. In those moments, I could simply be, letting go of the past, piece by piece.

Dear Mistress

I never imagined that my journey to inner peace would involve the guidance of such an extraordinary woman, a disciplinarian Mistress who seemed more like an enigma than a person. At first, I was sceptical, hesitant even, unsure of what her role in my life might be. But from our very first session, she became a pivotal force, her presence unravelling parts of me I had long hidden.

She carried herself with a confidence that was magnetic but never overbearing. Articulate and well-spoken, she had a way of choosing her words as if each one were a gift, deliberate and meaningful. Her voice was warm and low, calming yet commanding, the kind of tone that made you stop and truly listen. There was no pretence in her demeanour, no sense of superiority or judgment. She saw through people without reducing them and understood flaws without condemning them.

Her presence was undeniably powerful, not in a loud or aggressive way, but in the quiet strength that radiated from her. It was as if she embodied every aspect of femininity: nurturing yet fierce, tender yet unyielding. She drew people into her orbit without effort, a force of nature wrapped in grace. Even her movements were deliberate, imbued with a sense of purpose. She carried an aura that made you want to be better, not for her approval but because she showed you the person you could become.

In our sessions, she created a space unlike any I had known. It was a place where I felt entirely seen, where I could shed the masks I wore in the outside world. The vulnerability she drew out of me was not forced; it was invited. Her warmth allowed me to step into my truths, no matter how messy or uncomfortable.

She would begin each session with a quiet moment, her eyes meeting mine with an intensity that was both disarming and comforting. "How are you today?" she would ask, and unlike the rote pleasantries exchanged in daily life, her question demanded honesty. And I found myself answering, truly answering.

She listened with an attentiveness that felt like a luxury. There was no rush, no interruption, no attempt to fix or solve. Her listening alone was its kind of healing. "You don't need to justify how you feel," she'd say when I stumbled over my words, trying to rationalise my emotions. "Just feel it. That's enough."

As our sessions progressed, I began to see how much of my life had been spent suppressing myself, my voice, my emotions, and my needs. With her, I was allowed to take up space, to express myself without fear of judgment or rejection. She helped me untangle the knots inside me, not by solving my problems for me but by showing me that I had the strength to face them.

When discipline entered the sessions, it was never cruel or punitive. It was a practice, a ritual that grounded me in my own body and being. She explained each step with care, ensuring that I understood it was not about shame or guilt but about release and transformation. "This is your time," she'd remind me. "Your choice. Your process."

And it was always my choice. This was something she emphasised from the beginning. Her words empowered me, reminding me that even in moments of surrender, I held the reins.

One of the most poignant moments of each session came near the end when she would let me choose the cane to close with. It seemed like a small act, but it carried weight, a reminder that even in moments of discomfort, I had agency. On a small table in the corner of the room, the canes were neatly stacked, each one laid with care, each one different in its size and weight. And her eyes would meet mine with steady patience.

"Take your time," she'd say softly.

I'd run my eyes over them, taking in their smooth surfaces and the promise they held. It wasn't about pain but about release, a way of shedding what I had carried into the room. When I finally chose, she would nod in quiet approval, her respect for my choice palpable.

The moments that followed were intense, yes, but also cathartic. And afterward, as the session came to a close, she would step close and embrace me. The hugs were never rushed, never obligatory. They were firm, grounding, her arms a safe harbour where I could finally let go.

It was in those hugs that the tears would come, starting slowly, sometimes giving way to deeper sobs. She comforted me with a few words, without trying to fill the silence. She simply held me, her presence a quiet reassurance that it was okay to break, to feel, to be human.

In her presence, it felt safe to cry. Not the muted, hidden tears of shame but the raw, unfiltered kind that cleansed something deep inside. Each tear felt like a piece of the burden I'd carried for so long falling away.

When we finally parted, there was no fanfare, no need for long goodbyes. She would smile softly, her eyes filled with a warmth that lingered long after I left the room. And as I walked away, lighter than I had felt in years, I would marvel at the impact she had on my life.

I had come to her seeking structure, perhaps even punishment, but what she gave me was something far greater. She gave me back to myself.